DATE DUE	
NOV 6 2008 MAY 4 2012		

F   CIRCLE OF GRACE

GOU   GOULD, LESLIE

CIRCLE OF GRACE

HOME TO HEATHER CREEK™

CIRCLE OF GRACE

Leslie Gould

Guideposts
NEW YORK, NEW YORK

Home to Heather Creek is a trademark of Guideposts.

Copyright © 2008 by Guideposts. All rights reserved.

No part of this publication may be reproduced, stored in a retrieval system or transmitted, in any form or by any means, electronic, mechanical, photocopying, recording or otherwise, without the written permission of the publisher. Inquiries should be addressed to the Rights & Permissions Department, Guideposts, 16 E. 34th St., New York, NY 10016.

The characters and events in this book are fictional, and any resemblance to actual persons or events is coincidental.

Scripture quotations marked (NLT) are taken from the *Holy Bible*, New Living Translation. Copyright © 1996. Used by permission of Tyndale House Publishers, Inc., Wheaton, Illinois 60189. All rights reserved.

www.guideposts.com
(800) 431-2344
Guideposts Books & Inspirational Media

Cover by Lookout Design, Inc.
Interior design by Cindy LaBreacht
Typeset by Nancy Tardi
Printed in the United States of America

Acknowledgments

I'm very grateful to Sallie Beth Fisher, Emily King, and Dori Clark for sharing their insights into being grandmothers. These three lovely women are the heart behind my Charlotte.

My thanks, also, to Susan Ritta for answering my questions about life in Nebraska, Elizabeth Salter for being my first reader, and to my editor Beth Adams for an amazing job on this particular book and the entire Home to Heather Creek series.

Finally, thank you to my family for your ongoing support and inspiration.

—Leslie Gould

Chapter One

Charlotte Stevenson stepped from the dim chicken coop into the first light of morning. Dodging the pecking hens and crowing rooster, she crossed the yard. Overhead, hundreds of geese flew south over the farm, soaring over the barn, the horse pasture, and the fields of ripe corn. She tilted her face to the perfect formation of the birds, remembering that she had read, years ago, that geese journeyed in family groups, the young and the old all together, encouraging each other on.

She pulled her corduroy work coat tight against the chill with one hand as she clutched the handle of a plastic pail of eggs with the other. Ahead, her century-old house was lit up like a jack-o'-lantern against the peach-colored horizon as light spilled through every windowpane, upstairs and down. Her three grandchildren were getting ready for school, right on time.

Sixteen-year-old Sam might be showering. Emily, who was a month into her first year of high school, would be primped and eating breakfast by now. Ten-year-old Christopher was probably distracted by a book, maybe the one on natural disasters that he had picked up at the library yesterday.

A slight breeze rustled through the golden cornstalks in the field, and the honking of the geese grew fainter as they flew high above the cottonwoods that lined Heather Creek.

Charlotte hurried toward the garden. Giant sunflowers and purple dahlias swayed in the morning breeze, and late zucchinis inched over the soil and onto the lawn. A handful of almost-red tomatoes clung to their vines. Toby barked from the backyard and ran toward Charlotte. She petted the dog's neck, and in return received a few quick licks and wet-nose kisses. It was a perfect morning. Cold and dry, but holding the promise of October-in-Nebraska warmth.

She opened the backdoor, slipped her boots onto the worn linoleum, and hung her coat on a wooden peg.

"What's with the granola?" Charlotte's thirty-two-year-old son Pete poked at the cereal box in front of Emily. "We're a cornflakes family. Remember, we grow corn." The two sat at the kitchen table. Pete, even though he had a perfectly fine kitchen in his apartment above the shed, ate nearly every meal with the family, especially since the children had arrived just over five months before.

Emily tossed her long blonde hair over her shoulder. "Get over it, Uncle Pete." She grinned and then turned her attention to her grandmother. "How's Stormy doing?"

"Just fine." Charlotte lifted eight brown eggs from the pail to wash. Usually Emily fed the chickens and tended the horses, including the foal, but she had an algebra exam that she had stayed up late studying for, and Charlotte had let her sleep a half hour extra.

"Grandma." Emily's tone changed. "Are you going to wear that old shirt all day?"

Charlotte brushed a permanent stain on the sleeve of her faded pink blouse. "As a matter of fact, I am."

"Oh." Emily turned her attention back to her granola.

Charlotte patted her short, brown hair. Had she combed it before she headed out to the barn? Yesterday Emily asked when Charlotte planned to start dyeing her hair. Charlotte had laughed, thinking Emily was joking. But Emily seemed to think every woman should dye her hair, especially someone with as much gray as Charlotte. There was nothing like having a teenage girl in the house to make a woman feel self-conscious about her looks.

"Grandma, have you seen my backpack?" Christopher bounced on one foot. His close-cropped blond hair stuck up at the crown, and his long-sleeved T-shirt looked as if he'd slept in it.

"Check by the front door." Christopher could be as absent-minded as a teenager. "And don't forget to feed Toby."

"I already did, when I first got up."

Of course he'd already fed the dog. Toby was on her way to becoming Christopher's new best friend. He'd feed her at the table if he could.

"How about your kitten?"

"Lightning still has food," Christopher answered.

Actually, Lightning wasn't much of a kitten anymore. As if on cue, the half-grown cat slinked between Charlotte's feet, his tail winding against her leg as she pulled the straining cloth from the cupboard above the sink. Pete had done the milking and left the full stainless steel pail on the counter. She shooed Lightning away.

"But you still have to eat," she said, nodding at Christopher.

"In a minute," he said as he disappeared down the hall.

"Is Dad up?" Pete poured coffee into a travel mug and sat it on the counter.

"He was awake when I headed out to the barn." Charlotte pulled a loaf of bread from the cupboard.

"'Cuz we start on the corn today." Pete turned to Emily. "Corn, not granola." He swept his John Deere baseball cap off his head and bowed from the waist.

Emily giggled. "You look like the scarecrow in *The Wizard of Oz*."

"That's me." Pete ran his hand through his dark hair and then replaced his hat with a flourish as he sang, "If I only had a brain..."

Charlotte strained the milk. Denise had loved *The Wizard of Oz*. She used to force Pete to watch it with her whenever it showed on TV and then they would act it out for days afterward. Did he remember? Perhaps Emily had watched the movie with her mother too.

"Is Sam up?" Charlotte asked Emily.

"I think he's shaving." Emily giggled again. "In the downstairs bathroom."

"This, I've got to see." Pete bolted from the kitchen.

"Grandma, can Ashley come over Friday, after school?"

"Sure, honey, as long as you're caught up with your chores and homework." Charlotte spread peanut butter on the whole-wheat bread. Sometimes all it took was one good friend to keep a girl on the right track. She opened the pantry door and retrieved a jar of homemade apple butter and then pulled out a container of roast beef from the fridge for Sam's lunch.

Emily rolled her eyes. "How can he eat that stuff? Especially now that he actually knows—"

"Mom!" It was Pete, coming down the hallway.

The tone in his voice made Charlotte hurry to the doorway. "What's wrong?"

"Dad's still in bed."

"Is he okay?"

"He says he's all right, but he's not getting up."

"Maybe his blood sugar is low."

"Maybe you should go talk with him. He started to get defensive with me."

Charlotte started down the hall. Pete had no idea what it was like to get old.

"He's the one who didn't want to hire a crew to do the corn," Pete said. As he headed back to the kitchen, Pete called over his shoulder, "He'd better be able to pull his weight."

Charlotte sighed. Bob had been adamant about doing the corn harvest themselves, and it didn't seem to be as much about money as pride. "We're farmers," he had said. "We farm. We harvest. That's what we do."

Emily's laughter floated down the hall, followed by Pete's loud good-bye, and the slam of the backdoor.

Sam stood at the bathroom sink, dabbing at his rosy face with a hand towel, his dark hair wet and wavy from the shower.

Charlotte called out good-morning and hurried on down the hall, opening her bedroom door, softly. "Bob, are you feeling all right?" She stopped at the end of their four-poster bed. "Have you checked your blood sugar?"

Bob flung his legs over the side of the bed. "I'm fine. I just fell back asleep, that's all."

"Are you sure?"

Bob waved Charlotte away as he reached for his robe.

"I'll start your eggs." Charlotte closed the door behind her.

She finished packing the children's lunches and then cracked two brown eggs into a dented metal bowl. She'd been fixing eggs for Bob most mornings for forty-five years.

Emily stood in the doorway and tugged on her thin shirt. Her top was too skimpy and her pants were too low, but Charlotte refrained from asking her if she was cold.

"I need to stop by Fabrics and Fun today. Do you need anything?" Charlotte asked. She thought it best for a teenage girl, any girl, to have a project to keep her busy.

Emily fingered the hem of her shirt. "I'm too busy right now. Algebra is taking up most of my time."

Charlotte tilted her head. *When did Emily become so concerned about algebra?* she wondered as she poured the eggs into a cast iron skillet while Christopher dragged his Spider-Man backpack into the kitchen.

"What's in that thing?" Charlotte asked. "Bricks?"

"Books." Christopher had a serious look on his face as he poured cornflakes into a bowl and then splashed milk on top.

"I saw a flock of geese this morning," Charlotte said. Of all of her grandchildren, Christopher was the one who was the most interested in nature. "Several flocks, in fact."

Christopher didn't answer.

"They're beating the weather, going south." Charlotte turned toward her grandson.

"To California?" Christopher held his spoon in midair, dripping milk onto the table.

"Probably not. More likely Texas or Mexico." Charlotte wiped up the milk with a dishcloth.

Christopher took another bite of cereal and then another, shoveling the cornflakes into his mouth. He finished and hurried to the sink, sloshing milk onto the floor. Charlotte handed him a rag from under the sink.

"Grandma." Christopher kneeled on the linoleum. "What do the geese do if there's a tsunami?"

Charlotte laughed. "There aren't any tsunamis around here."

Christopher looked exasperated with her. "In California."

"Oh, I don't know. Fly inland probably." Charlotte rinsed out the rag.

"Can they sense it coming?"

"Maybe. Animals and birds can sense a lot of things." Charlotte patted the top of her grandson's head, but he flinched and pulled away.

Sam slid into the kitchen carrying his shoes and backpack. "We'd better get going." He grabbed a banana from the fruit bowl and stuffed it into the pocket of his sweatshirt.

"You need more breakfast than that."

Sam grabbed three granola bars from the pantry. "Emily, we're leaving," he called out as he shoved his feet into his shoes.

"I'm coming."

Emily retrieved her denim jacket from the peg by the back door and picked up her schoolbag, stuffing her algebra book inside. "There's a new girl at school. She sits by me in algebra. I've decided to be her friend."

Charlotte turned off the stove burner, warmed that Emily, so new herself, was reaching out to others. "Sweetie, that's great. What's her name?"

"Rayann."

Sam opened the backdoor. "There's a new boy too."

"Really?" Charlotte slid Bob's eggs onto a plate.

"He drives a Mustang. He's from Lincoln. And he thinks he's hot—" Sam paused.

Charlotte shot him *the* look.

"—stuff."

"We're going to be late." Emily waved as she shoved her brother out the door.

Christopher jerked his Spider-Man backpack off the chair and followed.

"And, get this." Sam filled the doorway again. "The new boy is Rayann's brother. That's why Emily wants to be—"

"Sam!" Emily yanked her brother into the yard and slammed the door behind them.

Charlotte stood at the kitchen window. Emily chased Sam across the lawn, Toby barked as she ran beside Christopher, and a flock of geese flew over the farm, over the awakening land.

A moment later only the garden, the ripe fields of corn, and the blue sky remained.

Chapter Two

Charlotte double-checked her watch as she turned her Ford Focus onto Lincoln Street. *2:15*. She would stop by Kepler Pharmacy, cross the street to Fabrics and Fun, and then maybe have time to dash over to Mel's Place for a quick cup of coffee before she headed home to meet the bus.

The pharmacy smelled like a mix of iodine, lotion, and the dusty stuffed animals that filled an entire row of the store. Charlotte was sure some of them were the same animals Denise had coveted when she was a girl. A fluorescent light overhead flickered and then began to buzz as Charlotte approached the prescription counter. The pharmacist met her with Bob's Glucophage in his hand.

"Thank you." Charlotte pulled her wallet from her purse. "So far these are doing the trick."

"Glad to hear it." The pharmacist slid the bottle of pills into a bag. "Bob's lucky he doesn't have to give himself shots."

Yet. Charlotte pulled out her debit card.

The door buzzed and Pastor Nathan waved as he hurried into the store. "Hi, Charlotte. I was just thinking about you and the children."

Charlotte hugged her pastor.

"How is everyone?" Nathan pushed his wire-rimmed glasses higher on his nose.

"Just fine." Charlotte took her card, the receipt, and the bag from the pharmacist.

"Wonderful." Pastor Nathan clasped his hands together.

Charlotte nodded. "I think that we've turned a corner."

"You don't say." Pastor Nathan walked toward the door with her. "You know, I've been wanting to talk with you about Sam; I saw him kicking a soccer ball around yesterday during lunch. Sometimes I stop in and have lunch with Nancy after the students have been served."

Charlotte nodded. Nancy, Pastor Nathan's wife, worked in the school cafeteria.

"Boy, does that kid have a powerful foot. He should have gone out for the football team as a kicker." Pastor Nathan held the door open. "Wouldn't that be great for Sam?"

Charlotte nodded, but she couldn't fathom Sam playing football. That was one of the things he liked least about Nebraska. Everyone was into football; Bedford didn't even have a soccer team. She didn't want to explain all that, though. "I don't know if his grades are good enough," Charlotte said, which was true too.

"Ah, how're his studies coming along?" the pastor asked.

"Better." At least she hoped so. Charlotte put the pharmacy bag in her purse.

"Good." Nathan paused and then continued. "You know, I majored in history before I went to seminary, and I've done quite a bit of writing in my life." He smiled. "I'd be happy to help."

"Thank you." Charlotte said her good-byes and headed

across the street, wondering if Sam would be willing to be tutored by Pastor Nathan. It was hard to tell.

Pictures of pumpkins and autumn leaves and a *Sale!* sign decorated the windows of Fabrics and Fun. A blast of lavender potpourri greeted Charlotte as she hurried through the door.

"Char!" Rosemary hurried from behind the counter, her steel-gray hair bouncing a little with each step. She hugged Charlotte. "How's my *little* bro doing?" It was one of her favorite jokes. Bob was Rosemary's younger brother, by eighteen months, but he was quite a bit bigger.

"He's working too hard." Charlotte rolled up the sleeves of her blouse. The afternoon had grown warm. "He gets tired but won't admit it. He could hardly get out of bed this morning."

"Remember how Dad kept working like that?" Rosemary stacked bolts of orange fabric on the counter. "How it drove Bob crazy?"

Charlotte nodded. Her father-in-law worked on the farm until the day he died.

"We have a new shipment of embroidery floss." Rosemary nodded toward the first aisle, changing the subject abruptly. "And it's on sale."

"Great, that's exactly what I need." Charlotte slung her purse strap over her shoulder and followed her sister-in-law to the embroidery section. "I was also wondering about a sewing project for Emily, something for her to enter in the fair next year. I thought it might be—" Charlotte almost said *fun*, but that wasn't the right term— "a good experience for me to teach Emily to sew."

Rosemary stopped in front of the row of floss. "Not very

many girls sew anymore. They do things like 'Decorate Your Duds.'"

Charlotte shook her head. What was Rosemary talking about?

"You know. Embellishing stuff, like jean jackets with rhinestones, that sort of thing."

Charlotte couldn't imagine Emily putting anything like that on her jacket.

"Though Lily Cunningham entered a dress in this year's fair. I think she's a freshman." Rosemary dropped her voice to a whisper. "A little slip of a dress." Charlotte visualized a skimpy little garment, just the thing Emily would choose. "Girls used to sew because it was less expensive than buying an outfit." Rosemary pulled on both ends of the tape measure around her neck.

"Do you remember that sundress and bolero jacket that Denise made?" Charlotte's voice wavered, just a little, as she said her daughter's name, but then she remembered that Denise had hated both the pattern and the process and she wanted to smile. It was Charlotte who had coerced her into sewing it. "I'll ask Emily. She's busy with school right now, but maybe once she gets the hang of it she'll have more time." Charlotte turned her attention to the embroidery floss and pulled a skein of royal purple from the rack. She planned to embroider a pillowcase for each of the children for Christmas.

"How's your quilting coming along?" Rosemary asked.

"I haven't had time to quilt. That's why I'm getting back to embroidering." There was no way that Charlotte could make quilts for the children by Christmas; pillowcases would have to do.

"I rearranged the linens last week." Rosemary started to the back of the store. "How about patterns? Do you need some new ones?"

"No, I'm good." Charlotte winced. The kids were definitely influencing her speech. "I just need three pillowcases and—" she pulled emerald green, midnight blue, and metallic gold from the rack, "—these colors." She would use a nativity-scene pattern that she'd embroidered for her own children nearly thirty years ago.

"So things really are going well?" Rosemary asked as she rang up Charlotte's purchases.

Charlotte nodded. "Sam seems to be doing his homework, Christopher seems a little more secure, and, listen to this, there's a new girl at school that Emily has decided to befriend."

Rosemary slipped the thread and pillowcases into a bag. "Is it Margaret Matthews's daughter?"

Charlotte shook her head. She couldn't place Margaret Matthews. "The girl's name is Ray—Ray something." Charlotte handed Rosemary her debit card as she tried to recall the name.

"Rayann." Rosemary ran the card through the slot in the cash register.

"That's it. Do you know them?"

"Margaret is Sig Campbell's daughter."

"Peggy? And she has a daughter Emily's age?" Peggy had been between Denise and Bill in school. She'd been head cheerleader and homecoming queen, a petite little thing with a lot of spunk.

Rosemary nodded. "She has an older boy too."

"That's what Sam said." Charlotte took her bag.

"Margaret came home to take care of Sig because he's failing pretty fast. I heard she had to force the kids to come with her. Both wanted to stay in Lincoln." Rosemary crossed her arms. "Guess Rayann has that in common with Emily, huh? Feeling displaced."

Charlotte nodded. She hoped Emily was past feeling that way. She had a good friend in Ashley. She seemed to be more settled. She thanked Rosemary and hurried out the door, checking her watch as she started across the street. She had fifteen minutes until she needed to leave town to meet the bus, just enough time for a cup of coffee at Mel's Place.

Melody Givens vigorously scrubbed a table in the back of the café as Charlotte hurried through the door. A year ago, Charlotte only knew Melody as someone who'd gone to school with Denise. Now, thanks to Emily's friendship with her daughter Ashley, Melody was one of Charlotte's closest friends.

"Hi!" Melody wore a bright yellow blouse and a red apron with *Mel's Place* machine-embroidered across the front. She waved the damp bar towel in Charlotte's direction.

"I have just a couple of minutes," Charlotte said. "I thought I'd grab a cup of coffee."

"Coming right up." Melody walked behind the counter, and Charlotte sat down and spun around on her stool. Miniature pumpkins, colorful gourds, and red, orange, and yellow silk leaves decorated the centers of the tables, and a new display of artwork lined the walls.

"Can you pick out Sam's painting?" Melody carefully placed the cup of black coffee in front of Charlotte.

Charlotte stood. "Which one is his?" Sam hadn't said a word about a painting of his being on exhibit.

"Straight ahead. The sunset."

Charlotte stopped in front of Sam's artwork. It was a beach scene with the shadow of a ball in the right-lower corner and a black bird, flying away, in the upper-left corner. Orange, red, pink, and pale blue bled into each other.

"It's good, isn't it?" Melody stood beside Charlotte.

Charlotte nodded, unable to speak. It was amazing how a piece of art could tell her more about how Sam felt than anything he'd said to her in the last six months.

Ashley swung through the door, red curls bouncing, calling out hellos to her mother and Charlotte.

"Why are you out of school early?" Charlotte sat back down at the counter and wrapped her hands around the coffee mug.

"Early?"

Charlotte held up her wrist. "It's only two thirty."

Melody nodded toward the clock above the door. "Charlotte, it's three fifteen. School got out ten minutes ago."

"Oh dear." Embarrassed, Charlotte stood. "I better get going." Why hadn't she figured out that her watch had stopped?

"The kids will be okay if you don't meet the bus." Melody spoke softly as she motioned to Charlotte's coffee.

"I know. I just don't want them to wonder where I am. Especially Christopher." She didn't want him to worry, to remember waiting for Denise.

"Emily won't be on the bus." Ashley pulled her curls into a ponytail and then reached for an apron on the hook by the door to the kitchen.

"Pardon?" Charlotte slung her purse strap over her shoulder.

"She's getting a ride with the new kids. They had to stop by the pharmacy for their grandfather's medicine." Ashley looped the apron strings around front and tied them. "They're parked out on the street."

"Oh." Charlotte headed to the door and then stopped. "The coffee—how much do I owe you, Melody?"

"Don't worry. It's on me."

"Thanks." Charlotte took another step. Why would Emily accept a ride home without asking? Charlotte pushed the door open and squinted down the street. A Mustang, with its top down, was parked in front of the flower shop. She started toward it. A girl with blonde hair sat in the backseat.

"Emily?" Charlotte called out.

The girl turned. Ashley was right; it was Emily. "Hi, Grandma." Emily's voice was a little too high, a little too perky. She pushed the front seat forward and opened the door.

The young man turned toward Charlotte and then stepped from the car.

"I'm Mrs. Stevenson."

"I'm Sean." He jerked his head, flipping his dark hair away from his eyes as he spoke, and then he extended his hand.

"Pleased to meet you." Charlotte shook his hand. He looked older than a high school student. He had sideburns and a tuft of hair on his chin, almost a goatee.

"My sister, Rayann, is a friend of Emily's." He nodded toward the pharmacy.

Charlotte held her right hand against her forehead, blocking the sun. "Emily, I'll take you home now."

A tiny thing, smaller than Emily, with long dark hair pranced toward them. She had to be Rayann—she looked just like Peggy Campbell had twenty years before. A smile spread across her face.

"You must be Emily's grandmother." She thrust out her hand. "I'm Rayann." The girl had intense blue eyes that danced as she spoke.

Charlotte took it gently.

Rayann squeezed, hard, and then turned toward Emily. "Guess you don't need a ride, huh?"

Emily shook her head.

"Maybe tomorrow." Rayann turned back to Charlotte. "So nice to meet you."

"Likewise," Charlotte answered. "Emily, grab your book bag. We need to get going."

A minute later Emily crawled into the passenger seat of the Ford Focus. "Sweetie, you need to check with me before you accept a ride home. Call from the office or from your cell phone if you have it with you. I don't want you to ride with people I don't know."

Emily nodded, but it wasn't until Charlotte turned off the highway onto Heather Creek Road that that her granddaughter finally spoke. "He's so nice."

Lost in thought, Charlotte asked, "Who's so nice?" And then cringed. She knew the answer.

Emily sighed. "Sean."

Chapter Three

Charlotte propped the rake against the oak tree and massaged her right elbow. Christopher sat at the picnic table on the porch, and Toby lay beside the bench. Christopher wouldn't make eye contact with Charlotte when she first arrived home, late, but now he seemed to have forgiven her.

"Grandma, I'm going to do a report on natural disasters."

"Oh." Charlotte slipped her glove back on her hand and resumed raking. "Have you cleared the topic with your teacher?"

Christopher opened his book. "Not yet."

Natural disasters seemed like a pretty intense topic for a boy who had gone though his own life-changing disaster so recently.

Sam banged out the front door, and Charlotte fought the urge to ask him if he'd completed his homework. He tossed a soccer ball down the steps and gave it a swift kick toward the toolshed. Toby followed, barking at Sam's heels.

"Come here, girl." Christopher stood and followed the dog.

"Pass with me," Sam called out to his little brother, shooting the ball toward him. Christopher stopped the ball and kicked it, but then headed back toward the porch, and Toby followed him.

"Come on, Chris." Sam flipped the ball into the air and bounced it off his head, dropping it at his feet. Christopher didn't turn around. Sam kicked the ball against the shed again, holding both hands in fists. Every day his shoulders seemed wider and his face squarer, more sharply in focus.

"Christopher!" Sam called out.

His brother ignored him.

Sam returned to kicking the ball against the toolshed door, once, twice, and then again, his lanky frame in perfect control. Christopher held the book to his nose. Sam slammed the ball again, even harder, and then headed toward the house.

Charlotte raked a patch of bright yellow leaves from the maple tree. "What made you decide to write about natural disasters?" she called out to Christopher as she worked.

He shrugged.

"Which ones are you going to cover?"

"Maybe just earthquakes, I think."

"Why?" Sam sat down on the steps with his soccer ball in his hands. "There aren't any around here."

"Sure there are," Christopher said.

"Actually," Charlotte said, "I can't remember any around here. There have been a few other places in the Midwest but hardly any."

"Really?" Christopher sounded incredulous.

"Well, Pete claimed we had one a few years ago in the

middle of the night, but none of us believed him." Charlotte leaned against the rake.

"What happened?"

"You'll have to ask Pete." Charlotte started raking again. "It's one of those cautionary tales." Pete had a whole collection of those kind of stories to tell.

"Grandma!" Christopher jumped from the bench. "Tell us."

"Ask your uncle." Charlotte sighed. Maybe writing about earthquakes was a way for Christopher to work through some of his fears. The phone rang as Charlotte raked.

"I've got it!" Emily shouted from upstairs. A moment later she yelled, "It's for me!"

Christopher put his book down. "Grandma, there isn't any information in this book about earthquakes in the Midwest."

"Not at all?"

He shook his head.

"It seems like there was one in Chicago not too long ago."

"It must not have been very bad." Christopher looked disappointed.

"No, it wasn't. Not like earthquakes in California." She used to worry about Denise and the kids, that an earthquake would happen while Denise was at work and the kids were at school, and that Denise wouldn't be able to get to them.

Sam kicked his ball into the air and then caught it. "I'm going to go see if I can help Pete and ask him about that earthquake."

"Sounds like a good idea. They're at the bottom of the home quarter." Charlotte handed the rake to Sam. "Would you take this to the shed on your way?"

Sam nodded, taking the rake as he lobbed the soccer ball onto the porch.

"Can I go with Sam?" Christopher closed his book. "Uncle Pete said I could ride in the combine."

"Is your homework done?"

Christopher stood. "My project isn't due for four more weeks."

Charlotte nodded. "Tell Uncle Pete and Grandpa that we'll eat at six thirty. We're having meatloaf."

Christopher wrinkled his nose. Charlotte was sure he'd lived off chicken strips and fries in San Diego.

"I'll need you two to clean up the dishes after dinner," she called after them.

They nodded and waved as they ran between the field, Toby barking beside them.

Chapter Four

Emily pressed her nose against the windowpane in the family room as she talked to Rayann on the phone for the second time that afternoon. Grandpa and Uncle Pete stood in the side yard, in the dim light. Pete pointed toward the field behind the shop.

"Did your grandmother calm down?" Rayann's voice was cheery.

Emily hesitated. "Yeah, she's fine now." Grandma hadn't seemed upset, not really.

"She's not as old as I thought she'd be, not nearly as old as my grandfather."

"She's okay." Emily hoped she didn't sound too immature. She didn't want to sound too positive, not when she'd just met Rayann, who seemed a little cynical, just enough to be appealing.

"Well, don't be pouty or anything. My mom wouldn't want me to get a ride with kids I didn't know either." Rayann had a good point. Emily wound her index finger around a strand of her hair.

Rayann kept talking. "So, be happy." Rayann chuckled. "You know, you want her to trust you, 'cuz I want you to come over Friday night."

"Tomorrow?" Emily took a deep breath. She'd asked Grandma if Ashley could come over, but she hadn't actually asked Ashley. She'd been distracted at school by Rayann—and by Sean.

"Say that you're going to study with your algebra partner."

"I don't know." Emily sat down in Grandma's rocking chair. "She'll probably figure it out."

"Figure what out?" Rayann asked.

"That I ditched Ashley so I could hang out with you."

"Ditched Ashley?"

"I asked Grandma this morning if Ashley could come over tomorrow night." Emily couldn't believe she'd done that. What had she been thinking? Even yesterday it was pretty obvious that she and Rayann were going to be friends.

"Oh." Rayann chuckled. "Well, Sean can help us study."

Had Emily been that obvious? Could Rayann tell that she was crushing on her brother? Emily's face grew warm.

"Help you study what?" Sean's voice came across the line.

"Algebra. Friday night." Rayann's voice was muffled.

Emily sat up straight. Butterflies began to flutter in her stomach at the sound of his voice. Well, not exactly butterflies. More like moths floundering around the porch light.

"I might be in Lincoln." Emily could barely hear Sean's voice.

"Really?" Rayann seemed surprised. "Since when?"

"Since I talked it over with Mom today." Sean seemed impatient.

"So you're just going to ditch me?"

Emily couldn't make out Sean's answer. She slumped back against the chair.

"Well, count him out." Rayann was talking to Emily again. "We'll have to figure out algebra on our own."

Oh, well. Emily still wanted to go to Rayann's house.

The back door slammed, and she heard Grandpa and Uncle Pete's voices in the kitchen. Emily rocked the chair forward and stood. "Hey, Rayann. I've got to go. It's time for dinner. I'll call you later, okay?"

She did need help with algebra because either in the last few days it had gotten a whole lot harder or else she'd gotten dumber. Rayann had taken it last year as an eighth grader, but was taking it again. Ashley had taken it as an eighth grader too and was now in geometry. Just one more thing that Ashley excelled at, besides attracting the admiration of every adult she knew.

There was something about Rayann that comforted Emily. Rayann was confident, even more so than Bekka, Emily's best friend in San Diego. And it seemed like Rayann knew how adults thought, how to phrase things so that grown-ups listened; even their algebra teacher paid attention to Rayann. And her hair and clothes were really cute, big-city cute, not Bedford boring. She was really gorgeous too, and it was funny, but Emily had felt prettier, not pretty but prettier, at school when she was with Rayann, when they were walking down the hall and sitting in the cafeteria and waiting for algebra to start, and even when Emily was walking by Sean's locker for the fifth time, pretending to get another drink from the water fountain.

"Time for dinner," Grandma called out.

SAM, CHRISTOPHER, and Uncle Pete clamored around the table. *"Please* tell us about the earthquake," Christopher wailed.

Uncle Pete winked. "Later, dude." He nodded toward Grandpa.

"Oh." Christopher slapped his hand over his mouth.

An earthquake in Nebraska? Emily shook her head as she pulled out her chair. Just the word *earthquake* made her miss California. Sam bumped into her, and she started to complain but then remembered what Rayann had said. *Be pleasant.* Emily smiled at Sam as she sat down.

"What's with you?" He plopped down onto his chair and smashed his napkin in his lap. Grandpa said the blessing and then Sam and Pete began shoveling food onto their plates. Emily took a baked potato and sprinkled cheddar cheese on it. The steamed broccoli looked good.

"So, little lady," Pete said to Emily, "how was your day today?"

"Good." Emily turned toward Grandma and raised her voice. "I had an algebra test, and I don't think I did so well. But now I have a study partner."

"Algebra." Pete snorted. "It makes my head hurt to hear the word."

"So you don't use it now, right?" Sam asked.

"You bet we do." Grandpa's voice rose. "I'm always setting up equations to figure out fertilizer, seed-to-acreage ratios, yield, and profits."

"I don't," Pete mouthed. "I let him do it."

Sam laughed.

Emily concentrated on being pleasant.

"So who is your study partner, Emily?" Grandma cut a baked potato in half and nodded toward Grandpa.

"That's all I get? Half a potato?" Grandpa shook his head.

"Poor Grandpa." Emily patted his rough hand, evading her grandmother's question.

Grandma shook her head. "Grandpa doesn't need our pity. Right, Bob? Besides, potatoes are high in carbs." Grandma passed the dish down the table. "Very high."

"Grandma's right. We want you to take care of yourself." Emily passed the broccoli to her grandfather.

"What's with you?" Sam asked, his mouth full of white potato flecked with green.

"Stop talking with your mouth full," Emily sneered.

Sam laughed, spitting a piece of broccoli onto the table, and said, "There's the Emily we all know and love."

AFTER DINNER, Emily reminded herself to be positive as she dumped the table scraps into the bucket for the chickens. She handed Grandma the milk pail and smiled.

The rooster flew at Emily as she hurried through the chicken yard to the coop. She flapped her arms at him and then dumped the scraps quickly. Ten minutes later, she opened the barn door and inhaled the fresh scent of hay. Trudy mooed as Grandma swiftly milked her, the streams hitting the sides of the stainless steel pail like musical notes.

Emily slipped through the back door of the barn to the pasture and started the water in the trough. Stormy kicked up her heels and trotted toward Emily with her tail high in the air. "Come here, girl," Emily called out. The foal nudged her head against Emily's arm.

"Is this what you're looking for?"

Emily looked up quickly, surprised to see Grandma there. Grandma stood on the other side of the fence with a small apple in one hand and the pail of milk in the other. "Take it." She tossed it to Emily.

The other horses meandered over. Grandma pulled more apples from her pockets. "Who's your algebra partner?" she asked Emily as she held out an apple to Britney.

"Rayann," Emily answered.

Grandma nodded.

"She wants to study tomorrow evening." Emily gulped and rubbed Stormy between her ears.

"What about Ashley? Isn't she coming over tomorrow?"

"I didn't ask her," Emily said. "Not after I did so bad on my algebra test."

"You already have your grade?" Charlotte raised an eyebrow.

Emily shook her head. "I just know I did bad, that's all."

Grandma frowned.

Maybe she wasn't buying it. "Honestly, I'm not getting it at all," Emily whined.

Grandma didn't respond, so Emily continued. "Rayann's really good at math. She said that we can study at her house."

"We'll see." Grandma picked up the pail of milk, and Emily stayed quiet. She knew it wouldn't do any good to plead with Grandma. "I'll call Rayann's mother to check with her. Then I'll decide."

Grandma turned away from the fence.

Emily wanted to complain. Why did Grandma need to check on everything? But she kept quiet.

Five minutes later, Emily walked toward the house. Uncle Pete, Sam, and Christopher kicked the soccer ball around under the light by the garage. Emily stopped, and Uncle Pete kicked the ball toward her. She passed it to Christopher.

"Tell us about the earthquake," Christopher pleaded, passing the ball to Sam.

Sam shot the ball to Uncle Pete, but he didn't trap it—it went right past him and smacked the garage door. Pete laughed.

"Well, believe it or not, back in high school, I was interested in geology."

Sam hooted. "You're kidding."

Christopher leaned against the garage, beside Uncle Pete.

Emily rolled her eyes. Guys talked about the weirdest things.

"Yeah." Uncle Pete paused. "Anyway, one night when I was driving home from town in Lazarus—but that's before I started calling the pickup that—and everything began to shake. I was sure it was an earthquake, that there was some undiscovered fault in the earth's crust that ran along Heather Creek, so I stopped the pickup and jumped down to the road."

"And?" Christopher asked.

"It looked like my truck had landed in a sink hole."

Christopher gasped.

Pete laughed. "It wasn't a sink hole. It wasn't even an earthquake. The axle on the truck had broken. I knew something was wrong with it—I just didn't get it fixed in time. That's the moral of the story."

"Ah, Uncle Pete." Christopher stood up.

"But there are earthquakes around here, little ones that we never feel. California definitely has us beat on that front though."

"On every front," Sam said.

Christopher nodded.

"Now that's not true." Pete kicked the soccer ball to Chris. "Not if you like wide-open spaces."

"Flat, wide-open spaces." Christopher kicked the ball to Sam.

"Endless, flat, wide-open spaces." Sam pummeled the shed door with the ball.

Emily started back toward the house and across the flat, wide-open yard. Maybe Grandma had called Rayann's mom.

IT WASN'T UNTIL AN HOUR LATER that Grandma got around to making the call, after she'd tucked Christopher into bed. Emily sat in the family room, pretending to be doing her algebra, but she'd finished her homework after school.

Grandpa dozed in his chair, clutching the remote control. Emily concentrated on Grandma's voice. First Grandma apologized for calling so late. It wasn't that late, only 9:15 according to the clock on the video player. Then Grandma explained the reason for her call. There was a pause and then Grandma said, "Oh, Sean will be in Lincoln. I see."

Emily couldn't hear anything for a minute or two, because Grandma was probably taking clothes out of the dryer or something while she talked on the cordless phone. Emily picked up the picture of Grandma and her mom from the end table. Uncle Pete said it was taken on her mom's sixteenth birthday. She was so pretty, with her long hair flowing around her face and her hazel eyes. People had told Emily for years that she looked like her mother, but Emily didn't think so.

Grandma's voice floated back into the room. "Thank you, Margaret. I appreciate your condolences."

Emily put down the photo. There was another long pause.

"I'll see you tomorrow then," Grandma said. Emily stood, collected her book and papers, and hurried upstairs, nearly knocking Christopher over on the landing.

"I can't sleep," he said.

She took his hand. "I'll tuck you in." She dropped her homework outside her door and hurried across the hall, pulling Christopher along. He sat down on his bed with a bounce.

"Get in." She pulled the quilt up to his chin and sat beside him, the way Mom used to sit by her at bedtime. "Go to sleep." Emily kissed his forehead, the way Mom used to kiss hers. Christopher pulled back and scooted further under the quilt.

Emily hurried across the hall and grabbed her cell phone off her dresser. If she opened her window and stuck her head out, she could sometimes get reception, especially at night. She dialed Rayann's cell.

"Hi, Emily," Rayann answered just as someone knocked on Emily's door.

"Just a second." Emily answered the door, thinking it was Christopher. It was Grandma.

"Hey, sorry, I have to go. I'll talk to you tomorrow at school. Bye." She closed her cell phone and tossed it onto her bed.

"Who were you talking to?" Grandma asked as she stepped into the room.

"Rayann. About algebra. You were on the phone."

Grandma looked at Emily's book, still on the floor outside her room.

Emily blushed and scooped up the book.

"Emily, don't use your cell phone to make local calls."

"But you were using the land line."

Grandma crossed her arms. "It's too late to be making phone calls anyway."

"I know." Emily stifled a yawn. *Be pleasant.* "But her mom doesn't care."

"I do." Grandma started to leave the room and then stopped. "I talked with Margaret, Rayann's mother."

Emily plopped down on her bed.

"She would like to have you tomorrow evening, but I'm leaving it up to you. If you feel that you've handled things properly with Ashley and that working with Rayann on algebra is in your best interest—"

Emily bounced up from the bed.

"Then I'm okay with you going to Rayann's to study tomorrow night."

"Thank you." Emily sat back down on the bed, trying not to seem too excited.

Chapter Five

"Christopher, come on!" Emily flung open the backdoor. "Let's do the chores."

Charlotte put her finger to her lip, attempting to quiet her granddaughter. "He's upstairs. He can't hear you."

"He's taking his time on purpose." Emily pushed up the sleeves of her jeans jacket. "And where's Sam?"

"You go ahead. I'll round up the boys, and we'll follow you down."

"He's probably at the stupid computer."

"Emily."

"First the dishes, now the chores. You really don't want me to go to Rayann's, do you?" Emily crossed her arms.

"Emily." Charlotte hung the dishtowel on the handle of the refrigerator. "This is what we do every evening after dinner."

Emily threw up her arms and huffed out the backdoor, slamming it behind her and then quickly popping her head back into the kitchen. "Sorry. I didn't mean to do that. It slipped from my hand."

"What's going on?" Bob called out from the family room.

"Nothing." Charlotte walked to the doorway. She wasn't

being totally honest. Something was definitely going on with Emily, but Charlotte just wasn't sure exactly what.

Bob sat in his chair, the TV blaring. "She can stay home if she keeps that up. I can find plenty for her to do here." Bob sounded the way he did when their kids were teenagers.

Charlotte patted Bob on the shoulder against the worn denim of his work shirt. "She's just anxious, that's all." He smelled faintly of Old Spice aftershave and, more strongly, of diesel.

Sam turned from the computer. "Anxious about studying algebra? Ha."

"Come on, Sam. We need to get the chores done." Charlotte motioned to her grandson. "Go get the kitchen scraps and take them out."

Sam headed toward the kitchen.

Charlotte knew Sam was right. Emily hadn't suddenly developed a crush on algebra.

"Isn't there a high school football game tonight?" Bob asked.

"It's out of town, in Ridgefield," Charlotte answered.

"Oh." Bob picked up the remote. "I wondered why Emily and Sam were hanging around here."

Back when their kids were growing up, Bob and Charlotte and the whole family went to every football game, whether it was a home game or an away game. Sam and Emily were barely interested in the home games, let alone the away ones.

Charlotte sighed. Why did she feel unsettled about Emily going to Rayann's to study? Why was she so unsure of herself when it came to the grandkids? Was it because times had changed? Or because she had changed? Or because she didn't want to repeat her mistakes?

Christopher came thumping down the stairs, wearing a thin T-shirt. "Have you seen my book?"

Charlotte shook her head.

"I can't find it anywhere."

Sam rushed into the family room and lifted Christopher from behind, propelling him into the hallway.

Christopher roared, kicking his legs.

"Hey, keep it down." Bob's deep voice reverberated from the hallway.

Charlotte hustled the boys outside. Toby tore around the corner of the house and followed Christopher, nipping at his heels. Charlotte lengthened her stride. Darkness eased its way across the prairie. A small flock of geese flew toward the creek bed, gently swooping below the willow trees. Their calls punctuated the coming night.

Pete was hunkered over the combine next to the shop. "Hey, Christopher, come hold the flashlight for me."

Christopher and Sam both hurried over to Pete.

"Dad's on his way to help you," Charlotte called out to her son.

"No need." Pete flipped his baseball cap around and squatted. "I'm doing fine."

Bob's heavy steps fell across the driveway. "Careful with those heads. I don't want to have to reset any."

Metal clanked against metal and then a wrench landed on Pete's foot. He yelped. Christopher handed the flashlight to his grandfather, and the boys hurried toward the trough.

As Charlotte opened the barn door, Emily turned off the

light. "I'm all done except for watering the horses. And the boys are going to do that, right?"

Charlotte stopped in the doorway. "That was fast."

"It wasn't that fast. You were just slow." Emily walked out. "And Pete said that he'd milk Trudy, to save you time."

Charlotte nodded as she pulled the door shut and latched it.

Emily was quiet for the first half of the trip into town, but then she began to talk, and Charlotte had to concentrate to keep up with her granddaughter's chatter. Rayann's parents were separated, and she lived with her mom but spent every other weekend with her dad. She would have stayed with him in Lincoln—Sean too—but their dad traveled a lot and their mom wouldn't agree to them staying, since they would be taking care of themselves most of the time.

"Of course not," Charlotte murmured.

Emily continued. Rayann was super smart and creative too. She was really good at art. "Much better than I am," Emily said.

"Oh, I doubt that." Charlotte turned toward her granddaughter. Emily rolled her eyes.

Did Rayann know as much about the Stevensons as Emily knew about the Matthewses? Charlotte drove to the end of Meadowlark Street and stopped in front of an old Victorian, one of the oldest in town.

"Where are we?" Emily asked.

"Rayann's."

"How did you know? I didn't tell you the address."

"Sig Campbell is Rayann's grandfather. I knew his wife, way back when."

Emily rolled her eyes again. "This town. I'll never get used to it."

Charlotte put the car in park. "Peggy, Rayann's mother—she goes by Margaret now—was in school just ahead of your mom."

"She *knew* Mom?"

Charlotte nodded, turned off the ignition, and opened her door.

"What are you doing?" Emily lugged her book bag onto her lap.

"Going in."

"Why?"

"To say hello. It's polite."

Emily didn't answer.

Charlotte followed her granddaughter up the wooden stairs to the porch. Before Emily could ring the bell, Rayann opened the door. "Emily! Mrs. Stevenson, so nice to see you. Come in." She wore a tank top with spaghetti straps, and her long dark hair was twisted into a bun on top of her head.

Years ago, Charlotte had attended an afternoon tea at the Campbell home, when Selma Campbell, a real take-charge woman, was still alive. It was a fund-raiser for the city library. The house still held the warmth of its matron but had grown shabby over time. The runner up the open staircase was worn, the window above the fireplace needed to be cleaned, and the burgundy drapes had faded.

"We're going to study in here." Rayann pointed toward the formal dining room. Sure enough, an algebra book was open in the middle of the cherry-wood table.

The dining room opened onto the kitchen and behind that, in what was once the sun porch, was a family room. Charlotte could see a big-screen TV against the far wall. "Is your mom available?" Charlotte asked.

"She's taking care of Grandfather, in the back bedroom. It's time for his meds."

"Oh." Charlotte stood still a moment.

"Grandma?" Emily said, quietly.

Charlotte gripped her keys. "I guess I'll go then. Emily, I'll pick you up by nine thirty."

"Nine thirty?" Emily and Rayann blurted out in unison.

"We have chores in the morning. We have to turn the cows out onto the east home quarter, into the stubble."

Rayann raised her eyebrows. "Sounds like fun."

Was she being flippant? Charlotte couldn't tell. But the girl's blue eyes were lively—they made Charlotte think of the girl's grandmother. Actually, Selma Campbell had been a bit of a busybody.

"Tell your mother hello." Charlotte stepped back toward the door. "I'll check in with her when I pick up Emily." Charlotte told the girls good-bye and headed for her car. *No sign of Sean.* So why did Charlotte feel so uneasy?

Chapter Six

Rayann's room had an orange comforter on the bed, but the walls had old-fashioned drawings of flowers and birds that gave the room away as the guest room it had been until a few days before. Clothes were already strewn over the end of the bed and on the dresser, and Rayann's backpack was opened in the middle of the floor, its contents spilling out onto the carpet. "So, who do you hang out with at school?" Rayann sat propped against the headboard of her bed.

Emily sat in Rayann's desk chair, spinning a little from side to side. "Mostly Ashley."

"Ashley?"

"Red hair."

"Tons of curls?" Rayann wrinkled her nose.

Emily nodded. Didn't Rayann like Ashley's curls? It seemed like everyone else did.

"And?" Rayann asked.

Emily shrugged. What was Rayann getting at?

"Is she nice? Funny? Crazy?"

Emily flipped her hair over her shoulder. "She's nice."

Rayann had an expectant look on her face.

"Maybe a little too nice. All the grown-ups really like her."

"Don't you hate that?" Rayann moaned. "So, like what does she do?"

"Oh, I don't know." Emily paused, hoping Rayann would go on to something else, but she didn't. "You know, she likes school and does really well; she likes church, even Sunday school. She's always polite. Never gossips about people."

"Oh, I hate that!" Rayann bounced off the bed. "I can see that—totally." She grabbed her hairbrush from her dresser. "Hey, do you ever wear your hair up?"

"Sometimes." Emily was relieved. She felt uncomfortable talking about Ashley.

"May I?" Rayann began brushing Emily's hair. "'Cuz you'll look a lot older with your hair up. *Très chic*. Hey, did I tell you I was taking French in Lincoln? And then we move here, where they don't even offer French. Can you believe it?"

Emily had already taken three years of Spanish in middle school; she'd never considered taking French. She sighed as Rayann brushed her hair. It felt good. She thought of when she was little, when Mom used to brush her hair every day.

"It must have been so cool to live in California," Rayann said. "Did you see any celebrities?"

"We lived in San Diego."

"But I bet movie stars go down there too. Right?"

"Famous people ate at my mom's restaurant sometimes."

"Your mom owned a restaurant?" Rayann twisted Emily's hair on top of her head. "You didn't tell me that."

"She worked there. In Old Town San Diego, for like forever." The famous people who went there were never anyone Emily had heard of though; they were old actors who didn't make movies anymore and retired politicians.

Rayann secured Emily's hair with a clip that she had retrieved from her desk. "Voila! Look in the mirror."

Emily stood in front of Rayann's dresser and smiled. Rayann was right; she did look older.

On top of the dresser was a wadded-up crimson Cornhuskers sweatshirt. Emily rubbed her hand against the fabric.

"Do you want to borrow it? I'm bored with it."

Emily nodded. "Where'd you get it?"

"It was my mom's. She went to school there, but she didn't graduate. She got married instead." Rayann laughed a little.

"Will she mind if I borrow it?"

"Heck no. It's older than the hills. I meant to give it to Goodwill."

Emily picked up the sweatshirt. Uncle Bill had gone to the University of Nebraska. Maybe her mom would have gone there if she hadn't gotten pregnant with Sam and then run off to California.

"Guess we'd better study, huh?" Rayann led the way back to the dining room where she picked up her book. "Let's go into the TV room so we can watch videos while we do our algebra."

Emily stuffed the sweatshirt into her book bag and followed Rayann, and they settled onto the sectional. "This stuff is pretty simple." Rayann opened her book as she turned the TV to a music video that was just ending. "The linear problems. We did that in my class in Lincoln."

They had just started their assignment for Monday when a petite woman, a little older than Emily's mom had been, entered the room. "You must be Emily. You look so much like your mom."

Emily ducked her head, embarrassed. She didn't want to talk about Mom. Mrs. Matthews must have sensed that, because she took Emily's hand and shook it gently. "I'm Margaret. And I'm very happy to meet you."

Emily nodded. "Happy to meet you too."

Then the woman turned toward Rayann. "Could you give me a hand, Rayann? I'm having a hard time transferring Grandfather to his wheelchair."

"I'll be right back," Rayann said, sighing.

Emily stood, stretched, and patted the top of her hair. She hoped that, besides looking older, she looked taller. Another video started on the TV. Emily turned away from it toward two photos on the bookshelf. One was of Rayann taken several years ago. Her face was round, and she wore her hair in pigtails. The other photo was of Sean. He wore his hair short, almost in a crew cut, and shiny braces covered his teeth. She turned the photo toward the light—

"Where's Rayann?"

Emily startled and replaced the photo quickly. Sean stood behind the sectional.

Emily stepped away from the bookcase. "Helping your mom."

Sean nodded and walked out of the room, and Emily sank onto the couch, feeling shaky. He had come back. And caught her snooping, looking at his photo. She snatched up her algebra book and opened it.

"How's the studying going?" Rayann asked, tilting her head as she came back and plopped down beside Emily.

"Fine."

"Is it easier to understand upside down?" A smile spread across Rayann's face.

Emily's face flushed as she righted her book.

"Sean said he'd come help us in a few minutes after he gets off the phone with his ex-girlfriend."

"Ex?"

"They just broke up." Rayann smiled. "I never liked her much. She's a drama queen, even worse than me." Rayann laughed.

Ten minutes later Sean came back into the TV room and Rayann scooted over, making room on the couch for him to sit between the two girls. "We've got the linear equations down," she said, glancing at Emily.

Emily nodded, her heart racing. "But we're having a hard time with the linear inequalities." She hoped she sounded like she knew, or didn't know, what she was talking about.

"Show me in the book." Sean didn't sound very enthusiastic.

They were watching videos when Margaret pushed her father into the room. "Grandfather is going to hang out here with you guys for a little while." She set the brake. "Dad, this is Emily Slater, Charlotte and Bob Stevenson's granddaughter."

Mr. Campbell smiled at Emily. He was small and thin with a plastic tube running into his nostrils and an oxygen tank hooked to the back of his chair.

Emily stood and took the old man's wrinkled hand. "I'm

very pleased to meet you," she said. She smiled. Poor guy, he looked like he was about ready to collapse.

"And young lady, I'm very pleased to make your acquaintance." He smiled again and then folded his hands in his lap. He wore a sweat suit and slippers.

"Rayann, would you take Grandfather back to his room when he gets tired? I'm going to sit out on the deck and call your dad. We have some stuff we need to figure out."

Rayann grimaced, just a little. Emily settled back down on the sectional with her two new friends.

"Great," Sean moaned. "He probably hasn't paid his child support this month. We won't be able to keep our cell phones."

"Shhh," Rayann hissed and reopened her book.

Chapter Seven

Charlotte stood in the middle of the kitchen, surveying the boys' after-dinner cleanup. The stove needed to be scrubbed, but besides that they'd done a good job. She began straining the pail of milk that Pete had left on the counter.

"What's there to snack on?" Bob asked as he lumbered into the kitchen. He opened the refrigerator and then the freezer.

"How about some popcorn?"

"I was hoping for some ice cream." He looked so hopeful that Charlotte felt a little bad when she shook her head.

"I'll make some popcorn." Charlotte pulled a box of "light" microwave popcorn from the pantry and placed one package in the microwave, and soon the buttery smell filled the house.

Bob retrieved the *Bedford Leader* from the family room and sat down at the table.

"Anything new around town?" Charlotte asked.

"Corn prices are still going up."

Charlotte knew that; she listened to the farm report twice a day.

"The football team isn't doing very well; they haven't won a game yet."

"Really?" Charlotte sat down at the table. "Pastor Nathan said he thought Sam should have gone out for the team."

The house shook a little as the boys thundered down the staircase. "We smell popcorn," Christopher said.

"Scrub the stove, both of you, and then come help yourselves," Charlotte answered.

"What did Nathan say?" Bob folded the newspaper.

"That Sam has a great kick."

"Who said that?" Sam stood at the sink, squeezing the sponge.

"Pastor Nathan. He saw you kicking the other day."

"You said you don't play football." Bob slapped the newspaper on the table.

"I don't," Sam said. "We've been playing in PE, and I was just kicking around during lunch." He started scrubbing the stove.

"I wish you would have given it a try. I bet you would have been great." Bob propped his elbows on the table. "I was a lineman in my day."

Christopher took the dishcloth and wiped down the stove where Sam had scrubbed it.

Bob kept talking. "And Bill. You know he was MVP back when they won state."

Sam and Christopher nodded in unison as they returned to the table, and Charlotte suppressed a smile. Of course they knew Bill had been MVP; the whole world knew. Bob couldn't comprehend that Sam could be a good soccer player but not want to play football.

Christopher reached for a handful of popcorn. Charlotte handed him a plate.

Bob scowled, scooped up another handful of popcorn, and headed back to the family room.

"Sam." Charlotte leaned toward him as he tossed a few pieces into his mouth. "I forgot to tell you yesterday that Pastor Nathan also offered to tutor you, in history or writing or whatever you need."

Sam wrinkled his forehead.

"He was sincere. He would really like to help."

Sam pushed back his chair. "I don't need any help." He and Christopher grabbed more popcorn, and then both of them left the room.

Charlotte checked the stove. They'd done a good job, except around the timer. She grabbed the dishcloth from the sink and began scrubbing the grease off the plastic cover.

Nine o'clock. Where had the time gone?

She headed toward the stairs, intending to check on Christopher before she left to pick Emily up, but stopped at the sound of something on the porch. Surely a raccoon wouldn't be that bold.

She pulled the lace curtain to one side and discovered Christopher leaning against the railing; his body arched upward, his head pointed toward the starry sky. She opened the door to the chilly air and stepped out onto the wide boards.

"A penny for your thoughts."

"What?" Christopher turned.

"A penny for your thoughts."

"What does that mean?" He let go of the railing.

"That I want you to tell me what you're thinking." Charlotte wrapped her arms around herself. Her light sweater was no match for the dropping temperature.

Christopher shrugged. He wore a thin T-shirt and no jacket.

"What's the matter?" Charlotte put her hand on his shoulder. She knew that nighttime was often the hardest part of the day for Christopher because he missed his mom the most then.

Christopher took a deep breath. "Nothin'." But then he said, "Sometimes I just feel like something bad is going to happen."

Charlotte pulled him close, too close, because he wiggled away. "I think that's to be expected, sweetie, considering what you've been through, but it doesn't mean anything bad *is* going to happen." She stood still for a moment, aware of his breathing. She imagined his heart racing, just a little. She hoped he would say something more, that they could have a conversation about how he was feeling, but he stayed quiet.

After a little while, he said, "I'm going to go listen to music with Sam."

"What music is Sam listening to?" Charlotte followed him into the house. Sam's music made the rock 'n' roll she had argued about with her own kids sound like elevator music.

"The regular stuff, the old stuff you don't mind."

Charlotte stood at the bottom of the stairs. "Get your pajamas on first and brush your teeth. And go to bed in twenty minutes. We have a big day ahead of us tomorrow."

"What are we doing?"

"We're going to turn the cows out into the stubble," Charlotte answered.

"Into the what?"

"The stubble. It's what's left after the corn is harvested like on the east home quarter, with the fence around it, that Grandpa and Uncle Pete just harvested."

"Oh."

"That way the cows are closer to the house and we can tag and vaccinate the calves, as we have time."

"That sounds like fun." Christopher started up the stairs.

"It is fun."

Charlotte stepped into the family room to tell Bob goodbye but stopped in the doorway. He was asleep in his chair and slouched over to the side. She would check on him when she got home too.

The moon sailed below the stars as she drove into town. Charlotte knew not to press Christopher about how he felt, though she did wish that he would talk more.

As she drove down the empty road, she thought through the next day. She and the kids would help Pete and Bob with the cows. In the afternoon, she would go to the grocery store; her grocery bill had more than doubled since the kids arrived.

She pulled in front of the Campbell place. The porch light wasn't on. Wearily, she made her way to the porch and rang the bell. There was no answer, so she knocked. Still no answer. After a couple of minutes she cracked open the door. "Anybody home?"

Of course someone was home. She knocked on the open door and then took a step inside. "Margaret?" She stood in the foyer. "Rayann?" Music from a TV show, she assumed, played loudly in the background. "Emily?"

Charlotte stepped into the dining room. The big-screen TV was on in the family room. She could see two heads on the couch, two heads side-by-side. "Emily!"

Her granddaughter turned toward her and so did the other head—Sean.

"Grandma!" Emily jumped to her feet.

"Where's Rayann?" Charlotte asked.

Sean stood. "She just wheeled Grandfather back to his room." His voice was calm and even.

"Why didn't you knock?" Emily's hair was no longer down long; it was high on her head, looped into a bun.

"Emily, I did. I rang. I knocked. I called out everyone's name. Everyone except for Sean's."

"I just got back from Lincoln." Sean shoved his hands into his jeans pockets. "I decided not to spend the night."

"Oh." Charlotte clenched her keys against her palm, forcing them into her flesh. "Let's go, Emily."

Chapter Eight

"Have some pancakes. And bacon." Charlotte put the platter on the table.

"Nah. It's too early for food." Pete leaned against the counter, cradling a cup of coffee.

"Where'd you go last night?" Sam asked.

"Places." Pete yawned. "Where's the little lady?"

Sam shrugged.

"It's not often that you beat her to the breakfast table."

Sam poured more syrup on his pancakes. "It's Saturday. She's in no hurry to see the cows."

Charlotte poured herself a glass of orange juice. Emily wouldn't talk the whole way home last night and then she went straight to bed.

Christopher banged into the kitchen through the backdoor. "Toby's cold. It must be eight below out there."

"It's thirty-nine degrees, to be exact," Pete said. "The dog has seen a lot worse and so will you."

Charlotte patted the chair next to hers. "It will warm up in no time, you'll see." Pete could sound like such a know-it-all.

Christopher clapped his hands together. "It never got this cold in San Diego."

Pete pretended to shiver and then laughed. "Where's Dad?"

"He's out already," Charlotte answered.

"Counting cows?" Pete asked.

"No. Doing chores." And probably getting frustrated with how long the rest of them were taking.

"How do we herd the cows?" Sam asked as he speared another pancake off the platter.

"The pickup." Pete said as he yawned again.

"No, seriously," Sam said.

Charlotte smiled.

"What about the horses?" Christopher dipped his bacon in his syrup. "Don't we ride the horses?"

"We could," Charlotte said. She, Bob, and Pete usually just walked around the pasture and, with Toby's help, got the cows to the road. Then Bob would drive his pickup behind the cows, following them to the field.

"I think Emily would like to ride the horses." Christopher shoved a forkful of pancake into his mouth.

Charlotte hesitated. It could work, herding the cows with the horses, although it certainly wasn't necessary. "It does sound like fun."

"What sounds like fun?" Emily came downstairs wearing her tightest jeans. Her legs looked like willow twigs.

"Well, looks like Sleeping Beauty finally awoke. Where'd you get your duds?" Pete asked, eyebrow raised.

Emily looked down. "Nordstrom. Fashion Valley Shopping Center, San Diego. I bought them with my babysitting—"

"The sweatshirt, not the jeans." Pete guffawed.

"Oh." Emily opened the refrigerator. "My friend."

"When?" Charlotte asked. She didn't want Emily borrowing clothes.

"Last night. It was in my book bag." Emily emerged with a yogurt cup.

"Algebra, huh?" Sam smirked.

"As a matter of fact, we did study algebra."

"With or without Sean?"

"Both." Emily sat down beside Christopher.

Sam pushed back his chair. "I told you Sean wasn't going to Lincoln."

"He did go. He just got back early."

Pete poured the rest of his coffee in the sink. "I'm going to go check on the fence around the home quarter and then I'll see all of you at the barn."

"We're going to ride the horses," Christopher told Emily. "When we put the cows in the field. Just like in the movies."

PETE RODE ALONG with Charlotte and the kids, and as they made their way to the pasture, Emily, wearing an old cowboy hat of Pete's over her braids, led the way on Princess. Christopher rode gentle Britney, looking confident and proud. Sam jogged alongside his brother with Toby bringing up the rear.

Bob drove by in his pickup and parked it across the road from the field. He leaned against the tailgate, waiting, his John Deere baseball cap pulled down low on his forehead and his arms folded across his coveralls. "Whose idea was it to bring the hay burners along?" he called out, looking straight at Pete.

Charlotte intervened. "I thought it would be fun for the kids."

"We'll use either the horses or the truck," Bob said. "I don't want to be driving around in there with inexperienced riders."

Charlotte hadn't thought about that. "How about if we try it with the horses? If we can't get the cows, then we'll come out and you can go in with the truck."

Bob nodded, with a scowl on his face. "Fine. I'll walk along and supervise."

Sam swung the gate open and Bob led the way.

"Let's head down to the far end of the pasture, to the group by the fence," Charlotte said to Christopher, urging Shania forward.

"I'll stay here and tell Sam what to do," Pete said, sliding off Tim. Then he muttered, "And keep as far away from Dad as possible."

Charlotte felt the muscles in her legs stretch against the belly of the horse and knew she would definitely feel her age in the morning, but being on a horse made her feel young, for now. She used to ride as a girl, and during Denise's early teenage years, Charlotte would ride with her daughter for miles and miles on Saturday afternoons, often along Heather Creek, until it felt as if they were nearly to the Kansas border. One time they rode all the way into Bedford.

A big Holstein calf with a white face kicked up his back hooves as Bob headed toward the back of the field. Toby ran toward the largest group of cows. Emily trotted ahead, confident on Princess, her crimson sweatshirt bright against the blue sky. Christopher held the reins stiffly and dug his knees into the side of Britney. She inched forward. He'd done fine coming down the road, but now, in the pasture, he seemed unsure of himself. He was funny that way, one minute confident and excited about something, the next apprehensive and fearful.

"Come on, girl," Charlotte prodded the old mare along. Britney began to walk.

"Does she miss Stormy?" Christopher asked.

Charlotte shook her head. Britney was probably happy for the break from her busy foal.

"We'll get between the cows and the fence," Charlotte explained. "Actually we'll just ride along while Toby does all the work. This is her favorite chore."

Christopher seemed to relax a little. Emily reached the fence and turned; Princess cut toward the cows. Bob waved his arms. Toby had a small group of heifers moving across the pasture toward the gate where Pete stood, waving his baseball hat. Sam yawned.

"Let's ride toward that group." Charlotte motioned to Christopher to follow her toward five cows that were huddled under the ash tree in the southeast corner of the pasture.

Emily and Toby were working together as a team. Boys *or* horses. That's what Bob's dad used to say. Get a girl hooked on horses, and she'd ignore the boys. Charlotte sighed. If only it *was* that easy.

Christopher bounced alongside her in his saddle, up and down, up and down. Charlotte rode through the cows. "Come on, girls. Let's go." The cows started to move, but the white-faced calf broke away from the group again and headed straight toward Christopher. Britney sidestepped. "Grandma!" Christopher yelled.

"Easy," Charlotte called out, turning Shania between the calf and Christopher.

Bob lunged after the calf, but it bolted to the left, back toward Christopher. Bob turned quickly, for an old guy, and faced the calf, waving his arms. The calf panicked and raced straight at Bob, knocking him off balance.

"Bob!" Charlotte pulled on Shania's reins, turning her around. As Bob fell to the ground, the calf tumbled over him.

"Dad!" Pete ran from the gate.

But Sam was there first, helping Bob to his feet.

"I'm fine." Bob stood and took a step. His leg buckled and he fell to his knees. He stood again and took a full step. "Really, I'm fine. The calf kicked me in the leg, that's all."

Charlotte slid from her horse. "Are you sure?"

Bob ignored her and rubbed his lower leg. "I'm going to be sore tomorrow, but I'll be fine." He rubbed his elbow.

"You're lucky he didn't step on your head," Pete said.

"Well, if I'd been in my pickup, none of this would have happened." Bob rubbed his hands together and started walking back down the fence line, toward the cows. "Let's get this done."

Charlotte remounted Shania and headed back to the strays and Christopher, feeling shaky. Bob was determined, but he was moving slowly, pointing Emily toward the stragglers.

Christopher said something, but Charlotte couldn't make it out, so Charlotte rode closer.

"Is Grandpa okay?" Christopher whispered the words.

"He's fine." She stopped next to Christopher. "Did that scare you?"

He nodded. "Was it my fault? Because I asked if we could ride the horses?"

"Oh no, sweetie." Charlotte wanted to reach out her arms to hug her grandson. "It's not your fault. Sometimes things just happen."

The strays moseyed past Charlotte and Christopher. Bob walked behind them, shooing them toward the gate.

"Come on, sweetie. Let's drive these cows." Charlotte rode beside Christopher, gently pushing the cows along. Ahead, Sam opened the gate, and Bob limped through it toward his pickup.

"Grandpa," Sam called out. "Can I drive your truck?"

Bob shook his head. "Nope. Not until your grades are up to snuff."

Sam turned back toward the field, frowning, and Bob climbed into the pickup and started the motor. Charlotte tried to catch Sam's eye, but her grandson had turned his attention toward Pete.

"Don't worry about it," Pete said, sitting tall on his horse, and then shrugged. The white-faced calf tore through the gate and ahead of the rest of the herd, and Pete turned his horse and galloped after him up the road. Sam ran behind his uncle in a cloud of billowing dust. Kids and cows. Bob's dad had also said that those were the two most unpredictable creatures in the world. As Emily moved the last of the old cows through the gate, Charlotte was sure he was right.

Chapter Nine

Charlotte stopped the shopping cart by the ice cream freezer and peered through the frosted glass.

Charlotte gestured toward the containers. "Pick out a pail of ice cream. One of the big ones, because I want it to last."

Emily scrunched up her nose.

"What's the matter?" Charlotte was losing patience. They'd been shopping for nearly an hour.

"Christopher likes chocolate chip cookie dough. So does Sam, but I don't." Emily slid open the door.

Emily made a face, and her hoop earrings swung against her neck.

"That stuff," she pointed to the tubs on the bottom shelf, "is bad for you. Corn syrup. Fake milk. It's full of all sorts of junk."

Charlotte squinted to look at the prices. The bad stuff was half the cost and twice the size of the good stuff. "Pick out one container, then." She sighed. "You decide. Good or bad."

Emily pulled a small carton of cookie dough ice cream from the freezer. "I guess I like this okay. It'll be gone by tomorrow though."

Charlotte added the amount to her calculator and totaled the cost: *$193.27*. She was going to have to find a job just to pay the grocery bill. Thank goodness they raised their own meat, milk, and eggs, and grew their own vegetables. She hadn't canned as much this year, though, because they'd eaten most of it fresh. She would need to plant a larger garden next year.

"What's the matter, Grandma?" Emily tugged on the front of the grocery cart as they walked down the freezer aisle and toward the checkout lines.

Charlotte shook her head. "Just tired, I guess."

"I'll put the groceries in the pantry when we get home."

"Thank you." Charlotte began placing items on the conveyer belt while Emily headed down to the other side to bag the groceries.

"Things have changed for you in the last few months, haven't they?" Sally Meyers, who had been in school with Pete, said as she ran each item over the scanner. "Fruit snacks. Cold cereal. Chips. It looks like you're keeping those kids happy."

Charlotte nodded. What about the fresh fruits and vegetables, granola and oatmeal? It wasn't all junk, not by any means. "I'm keeping your boss happy too." She took out her debit card.

Sally dragged a can of orange juice concentrate over the scanner, flashing her hot-pink lacquered nails.

"Believe me, we love big families around here." She checked the price of the mango that Emily had talked Charlotte into buying. "Did you know that Dana Simons is back in town?" Sally asked, tossing her long hair over her shoulder.

Charlotte nodded. "She's my grandson Sam's English teacher."

Sally shook her head. "Boy, life has a funny way, doesn't it?" She chuckled. "These grandkids of yours sure are lucky that you took them in."

Charlotte was getting pretty tired of hearing that. "No." She spoke quietly, hoping that Emily couldn't hear the conversation. "Bob and I are very blessed to be able to have them."

"Well, hopefully they'll all stay in school."

Charlotte ignored her, finished paying, and then helped Emily bag the rest of the groceries. Comments about Pete dropping out of high school still, after all these years, stung Charlotte. Bob had told her, over and over, that it had nothing to do with her, that it wasn't a sign of them failing as parents, that it was simply a choice Pete had made that they couldn't control. Still, not many Bedford kids dropped out of school, and people remembered the ones who did.

Thank goodness Bill had done so well. He was mayor of River Bend and a partner in his law firm, but the truth was they hadn't raised Bill any differently than they had Pete or Denise.

As Charlotte put the last bag in the cart, Emily took hold of the handle and pushed it into the parking lot. And talk of how lucky Sam, Emily, and Christopher were that she and Bob had taken them in? How many times had she heard that in the last six months? Did people think that she and Bob might have chosen not to bring the children home? Charlotte took a deep breath.

And how did it make the kids feel to hear people say that

they were lucky? *Please.* Their dad had left, years before. Their mom had died. They were taken in by grandparents they didn't even know. It was only by the grace—

"Grandma!"

Charlotte bumped into the cart.

Emily stood by the car, the grocery cart against her leg. "The back's locked."

"Oh." Charlotte fumbled for her key fob and pressed the unlock button.

Emily lifted the trunk.

Dark clouds gathered on the horizon. Maybe it was going to storm. Charlotte grabbed an overstuffed bag from the cart as someone called out, "Hey, Emily."

Charlotte turned. Sean pulled his Mustang beside them.

"Hello, Mrs. Stevenson." Rayann's lively eyes smiled.

Charlotte said hello and began packing grocery bags into the car. Emily hurried over to Rayann and Sean, returning to Charlotte a moment later. "They want to know if I can go into Harding with them, to see a movie."

Charlotte shook her head. "We need to go home."

"Grandma—"

"Emily, we can talk about it more in the car, but I don't want you to go to Harding with them. Please tell them no thank you."

Emily put one hand on her hip. Charlotte shook her head as she grabbed another bag, and Emily stepped toward her friends, leaning against the Mustang. The roar from the engine masked her words. A moment later Rayann waved to Charlotte as Sean backed out of the space and then accelerated through the parking lot.

"Emily." Charlotte rested her hand on the cart. "I already told you that I don't feel comfortable with you spending time with a boy. He's a senior."

"Rayann is a freshman, and a girl, in case you hadn't noticed."

"Emily." Charlotte put the last bag in the car. "Watch your tone. Besides, Sean seems to be part of the attraction."

"Not really." Emily climbed into the passenger seat of the car as Charlotte returned the cart.

Not really? Charlotte climbed into the car.

"I can't help it that he's Rayann's brother, that they spend a lot of time together." Emily flipped the visor down and examined her face and then pulled on the ends of both her braids at once and frowned. "Don't you think that's admirable, that they like each other so much?" She closed the visor.

"Yes, that is." Charlotte turned onto Lincoln Street. "But not relevant." She didn't want to go into the fact that she didn't know if Sean was a good driver or what movie they were going to see. That was irrelevant too. It didn't matter if he was the best driver in the world or if they were going to see *Snow White and the Seven Dwarfs*. Charlotte didn't want Emily going to Harding with them.

Pete passed them on the straight stretch before Heather Creek Road, honking his horn and smiling.

"I wonder what they went into town for," Charlotte said as she waved. They'd been working on the old truck when she and Emily left. Sam waved back. Charlotte assumed Christopher was with them, since they knew she didn't like him to be unattended on the farm, but she couldn't make out his head in the middle of the front seat. Maybe he had fallen asleep. She hoped not; she didn't want him up late tonight.

Emily crossed her arms.

"I wish Pete wouldn't drive so fast. He's setting a bad example."

"Grandma, you worry too much." Emily stared straight ahead.

Charlotte tightened her grip on the steering wheel. "Well, I have a lot to worry about. But you're right, I shouldn't."

Pete's truck shimmied a little as he took the turn onto their road. Charlotte couldn't fathom how Pete kept Lazarus going.

"You *know* Rayann and Sean's grandfather, and even their mother. You said that they're good people." Emily tugged on her earring.

"I knew their grandmother, I'm acquainted with their grandfather, and I have a good impression of their mom, but that doesn't mean I would let you go to Harding with them or with any other kids from school at this point."

"When?"

"When what?"

"When would you let me go?"

"Emily, I have no idea. It all depends."

Emily crossed her arms again. "You would not believe how trapped I feel."

Charlotte shook her head. Emily sounded just like her mother had twenty years before. Charlotte pulled up by the back door, and Toby poked her head out of her doghouse and then climbed out, stretched, and yawned.

"Guess who we saw in town?" Sam jogged over from the shop where Pete had parked next to the combine.

Emily ignored him.

"We saw—"

"I don't care who you saw." Emily grabbed a bag of groceries.

"Boy, do you have a bug up your—"

"Sam, help us with the groceries," Charlotte interrupted. *Those two.*

Sam grabbed two bags and followed Emily. "I saw Rayann and Sean."

"Ditto. They asked me to go to Harding."

Charlotte followed the kids into the kitchen.

"And?"

"Grandma said no." Emily shot a glance behind her.

"He's got a girlfriend, Em." Sam slipped by Charlotte, back outside, followed by his sister.

"Not anymore."

"Who says?" Sam handed a bag to Emily.

"Sean told Rayann."

"When?"

"Last night."

"I wouldn't believe either one of them," Sam said, hoisting a bag and hugging it to his chest.

Pete started over from the shop, holding a hose in one hand and a clamp in the other.

"Where's Christopher?" Charlotte asked.

"He stayed here with Dad."

"Really?" She started into the kitchen. "Christopher!"

"Shhh." Christopher's voice came from the family room.

There was Bob, in his chair, covered with an old afghan, and Christopher at the computer. "Don't wake Grandpa. He's all tuckered out. I've been keeping an eye on him."

Charlotte took a breath and nodded. "I thought you were with Sam and Pete."

Christopher shook his head. "I stayed here with Grandpa. I've been doing some research on earthquakes."

Charlotte stepped closer and squinted at the screen.

"You were right. They do have earthquakes in the Midwest, just not very often. There was one in the early 1800s in Missouri, though, that made the Mississippi River flow backward."

"Really?"

"For four days." Christopher pointed at the computer screen, which displayed the site of a Memphis newspaper.

"Well, isn't that something?" Charlotte said, patting Christopher's shoulder.

Bob woke up with a start. "What's the matter?"

"Nothing, Grandpa," Christopher said, closing the site. "Everything's fine."

Chapter Ten

Charlotte toweled off her wet hair and headed up the stairs, stopping at Emily's door. She knocked, waited a moment, and then opened the door. "Time for chores." Charlotte stepped inside and touched Emily's shoulder. Emily was still in bed but rolled over and faced the wall. Charlotte sat down on the edge of her bed and touched her shoulder. "Then church."

Her granddaughter moaned.

"Did your alarm go off?"

"I forgot to set it." Emily pulled the covers over her head.

"Well, rise and shine. Stormy's waiting for her breakfast," Charlotte said as she headed toward the door. "The horses have nearly overgrazed the pasture, so they all need hay today." Charlotte cast one last look at her granddaughter, buried beneath the covers, and walked out into the hallway. She poked her head into Christopher's room. His bed was empty. So was Sam's.

Charlotte looked around, then started down the stairs. Outside the window on the landing, something caught her eye. Bob stood at the open gate to the field. A group of cows mooed in the middle of the field. Charlotte pushed the window open.

"He's going thataway!" Sam, wearing his red-and-black-plaid pajama bottoms and Charlotte's coat, ran toward the lawn, and Christopher cut across to the garden, waving his arms. The calf, the one with the white face, lunged to the right, toward the uncut corn.

"Keep him out of the corn!" Bob yelled.

Toby cut behind the calf and turned him.

"Attagirl!" Christopher caught up with the dog.

Sam came alongside the calf, boxing him in. "Open the gate!"

"Grab his tail!" Bob shouted. His energetic display did not disguise that his limp was much worse than it had been yesterday.

Sam lunged toward the calf, making contact with the tail for a split second. "Gross!" he yelled, holding out his hand. Sam ran after the calf again, this time slapping his hand around the tail and holding it tight as the calf bawled and lurched.

"Good job," Bob called out.

"What's going on?" Emily came up beside Charlotte, wrapped in her blue quilt.

"Looks like the guys had a wake-up call from that calf."

Emily yawned. "Is Sam wearing his pajamas?"

Charlotte nodded and leaned forward.

Just before the gate, the calf lunged, knocking Sam off balance. It slipped away, and Emily squealed as her brother went down and landed flat in the mud.

"Dad gummit!" Bob ran forward, trying to block the calf. Charlotte could see that he was moving slowly.

"Grandpa! The gate!" Christopher jumped over Sam and

headed to the field, pushing the gate against another calf that was trying to break free. Two steers were behind him.

Charlotte started down the stairs. "Come on, Emily."

The two slipped into boots at the backdoor and ran across the lawn. The second calf was out, but Christopher had the gate closed on the rest. Sam wiped his muddy hands on Charlotte's coat. Bob leaned against the fence, breathing hard.

"Let's go around the house," Charlotte said to Emily. They ran through the grass, heading off the second calf before he reached the road. Toby nipped at his heels. "Go toward the road," Charlotte told her granddaughter.

Emily managed to turn the calf, and Charlotte chased him back toward the field.

"Open the gate, Christopher, but not too wide," Charlotte called out. He obeyed, and Charlotte let Toby drive the second calf in. Sam followed with the white-faced calf, this time twisting his tail hard as he forced him through the gate. He pushed the gate, and it latched with a clank.

Emily hugged her arms around her thin frame and giggled. "That was fun."

Bob jerked on the gate. It held tight, though the severe look on his face indicated that he didn't exactly see the humor in it. "We've got a hole somewhere or else a Houdini calf. I need Pete to walk the fence." Bob took a deep breath and leaned against the fence again.

"Let's go get breakfast," Charlotte called out to Bob and the children, eyeing her muddy coat. She'd put it in the wash once Sam took it off.

An hour later Charlotte stood at the bottom of the staircase, yelling for Emily to hurry up so they wouldn't be late for church.

Emily finally appeared at the top of the stairs wearing a very short skirt, black leggings, and a thin sweater. She hurried down, her flip-flops flapping against her feet.

"It's a little chilly for that outfit, don't you think?" Charlotte asked.

Emily shook her head. "I'll be fine."

As they climbed into the car, Sam turned toward Emily and said something under his breath.

"What did you say?" Charlotte asked.

"Ignore him, please." Emily fastened her seat belt.

"He asked Emily who she expected to see at church." Christopher scooted to the middle of the backseat. Emily had told him it was the safest part of the car and now he always sat there. Sam smirked as he climbed in beside his brother.

"Oh." Charlotte started the car. Who *did* Emily expect to see at church?

"HOW WAS SUNDAY SCHOOL?" Charlotte asked as she and Bob met the children on the front steps of the church.

"Kind of boring." Christopher wrinkled his nose.

"Mine was about temptation. Peer pressure," Emily answered. Sam wandered toward the front door of the church.

Charlotte turned toward her granddaughter, pleased that Emily was sharing about Sunday school.

"But it was really cheesy. 'Sometime someone might offer you a cigarette or a beer.' Half of my eighth-grade class back home had already tried cigarettes, or worse, and a lot of them drank, mostly with older kids on the weekends."

"Really?" Charlotte stepped back. What else did the eighth graders in San Diego do?

The organ music started as they walked into church and then down to the Stevenson pew, the one under the stained-glass window with Jesus and the children. Emily and Christopher slid in first, followed by Charlotte, Bob, and Sam.

A few seconds later Pete sat down next to Charlotte. As Pastor Nathan stepped up to the pulpit, a woman slid into the pew in front of the Stevenson family. It was Dana Simons, her dark hair pinned on top of her hair, making her look even taller than usual. Sam nudged Pete— he'd been showing up at church lately, ever since Dana had come back to town. As the pastor started to speak, another woman slipped down the aisle, a woman who looked a lot like Emily's new friend Rayann, except much older. Was it Peggy—Margaret Matthews? My, how time did march on. She was older than Dana by five or six or seven years, but still, she looked older than that. Maybe it was just the difference between a single woman and a mom, or maybe the past two decades had been hard on Margaret.

Emily turned her head toward the back of the church. Charlotte refrained from looking too, suspecting her granddaughter was looking for Rayann and Sean.

Sam nudged Pete, but Pete ignored him. Pastor Nathan said the opening prayer and then asked everyone to greet a person near them.

Margaret turned around in her pew and a smile spread across her face. "Mrs. Stevenson. Mr. Stevenson." Margaret shook Bob's hand and then held out her hand to Charlotte. Bob sat down with a thump and pointed at his leg. Charlotte nodded.

"And Emily." Margaret grasped Emily's hand next. "So good to see all of you."

"It's nice to see you, Mrs. Matthews," Emily said, craning her neck down the pew.

"Oh, please call me Margaret." She let go of Emily's and Charlotte's hands. "I tried to get those kids of mine to come, but they were determined to sleep in."

"Please tell them hello for me," Emily said in her most grown-up voice.

Miss Simons said hello to Sam, and Charlotte turned away from Margaret, tuning into the conversation next to her. Sam shook her hand but didn't say anything.

Dana turned toward Pete. "Hello."

Pete wiped his hand on his jeans, extended it to Dana, and muttered, "Hi." His face flushed, and he slowly turned away from Dana and greeted the people in the pew behind them. Sam did the same.

Charlotte took Dana's hand. "It's so good to see you." She wanted to apologize for Pete, and for Sam, and ask Dana how Sam was really doing in school, but she didn't even know where to begin. Instead she said, "You look so nice."

Dana blushed and looked down at the pew.

Margaret began talking to Charlotte again, apologizing for not being able to greet her on Friday. Charlotte smiled and thanked Margaret for having Emily over.

"It was my pleasure," Margaret said, and then added, "My father is taking up all of my time these days. It's nice for the kids to have some friends to keep them busy. He's failing fast."

Charlotte patted her arm again. "I'm sorry."

As they all sat back down, Charlotte looked down the pew at Pete. His face was red and his hair was askew, as if he'd run his hand through it one too many times.

The sermon was on Lazarus. As soon as he heard the name, Christopher elbowed Charlotte and whispered. "Uncle Pete's truck!" Charlotte flushed. Had the children never heard the story of Lazarus? Probably not. They hadn't gotten that far in the Bible storybook that Bob read from every evening.

Pastor Nathan read the scripture and then spoke about how much Jesus loved Lazarus and his sisters, how Jesus wept with Mary and Martha, about how Jesus said to take away the stone even though Mary said that her brother had been dead for four days, that his body smelled.

"*Ewwww*," Emily whispered.

And then, he said, Lazarus came out of the tomb walking. Christopher elbowed Charlotte and she took his hand. "Does this stuff really happen?" Christopher whispered.

Charlotte swallowed. It *had* happened, once. Was he thinking about his mom? Before she could come up with an answer, Pastor Nathan did.

"It's not often that Jesus brings people back from the dead anymore." Pastor Nathan took off his glasses. "He performed miracles centuries ago to establish his authority and this one, particularly, because he loved Lazarus, Martha, and Mary. He loved them the way he loves you."

Christopher let go of Charlotte's hand.

"Maybe you are hurting. Maybe you have lost someone who you love." Pastor Nathan looked straight at the Stevenson pew. "Know that Jesus has felt this too. Jesus weeps with you too."

Christopher looked away from Pastor Nathan. He kept his head down, then reached forward and took a pen from the back of the pew in front of them. He began doodling spaceships on the weekly bulletin. Charlotte bit her lip. She had never allowed her children to draw during the service, but she didn't say anything to Christopher now.

"Maybe there is something that holds you back, that binds you, that hides you in a tomb," Pastor Nathan stepped away from the podium. "He wants to heal you from that too."

Emily took the pen from Christopher and drew a tic-tac-toe grid. She handed the pen back to her brother. He started with an X.

Charlotte turned her attention back to the pastor, who began to pray that they would trust Jesus to free them from their tombs.

AFTER THE SERVICE Pastor Nathan stood outside the door of the church and greeted his congregation. "That was a wonderful sermon, Pastor," Charlotte said. "Didn't you think so, Sam?"

"Huh?" Sam took a step backward. "Yeah. I guess so."

Pastor Nathan took her hand and then Sam's. "Well, thank you. How is school going?"

"Fine." Sam blushed.

"Did your grandmother tell you that I would be happy to help?" Pastor Nathan smiled at Sam, who shrugged.

"I'm doing fine." Sam took a step away from Charlotte and the pastor and headed toward Pete's truck.

Charlotte grimaced. "Thank you, Pastor. Sorry about that."

Pastor Nathan waved her apology away, and Charlotte smiled and hurried after Sam, who was standing by his Uncle Pete. She would talk to him about his manners later. For now, she had another concern.

"Have you seen Christopher?" she asked Sam. Pete nodded toward the churchyard.

Charlotte squinted at the wrought-iron gate. None of the kids had wanted to venture into the cemetery last Memorial Day when she had taken lilacs to the family graves. Why had Christopher gone now?

"Christopher?" She called as she tiptoed around the plots. She saw his tennis shoe first, back by the largest "Stevenson" gravestone. He was leaning against the marker with his eyes cast downward. Apparently no one had ever explained to him that you don't walk, or sit, on a grave. It certainly wasn't something they had talked about the day of Denise's burial.

She put out her hand to him. He took it and stood. "I wish Mom was buried here."

Charlotte nodded. So did she.

"Why did we leave her in San Diego?"

"It seemed best, at the time." Charlotte put her arm around Christopher and led him toward the gate.

"That sermon was creepy."

Charlotte stopped. "Why?"

The sermon had comforted Charlotte. Jesus wept with her, and he wanted her to trust him—to trust him with the children, with Bob's health, with all the things she worried about.

Christopher shoved his hands into the pockets of his jacket.

"I'm sorry, sweetie. Do you want to talk about it?" She could see how the story of Lazarus could be hard for a ten-year-old boy who had lost his mom.

"No."

"Do you want to talk about how you felt yesterday, when the calf knocked Grandpa down?" *And the night before, when you said you felt like something bad was going to happen.*

Christopher shook his head, pulled away from her, and hurried toward Pete.

Chapter Eleven

On Monday morning Pete said he was determined to finish the home quarter by midweek, and Charlotte told him she would bring lunch to the field to save them time.

She filled a plate for Bob with leftover roast from Sunday dinner, mashed potatoes with just a drizzle of gravy, and green beans, and then made one for Pete, adding three peanut butter cookies to his. She filled two salad bowls with greens and fresh veggies, spritzing Bob's with a lo-cal dressing and covering Pete's with buttermilk-ranch dressing.

She covered the plates and bowls with foil and placed them side by side in a cardboard box, tucking napkins into the side, and then poured fresh coffee into the thermos.

The phone rang as she headed out the door. She wiggled back through the door and set the box on the counter.

"Grandma? It's Sam."

Uh-oh. "Is everything all right?" Why would he be calling in the middle of a school day?

"Can I stay and practice with the football team?"

"May I."

"That's what I asked."

Charlotte sighed. "What's going on?"

"Brendan Jackson, he kicks for the team, broke his foot. Coach Thompson said he wanted to see me kick."

Had Coach checked Sam's grades? "Is this what you want to do?" After all that talk about hating football, why would he want to play?

"I might as well try. It doesn't mean I'm going to play or anything. He just wants to watch me kick, that's all."

"Then go ahead and stay," Charlotte said. Maybe a sport would be good for Sam.

Before she had time to say good luck, Sam hung up the phone. She laid the receiver down, picked up the box again, and headed to the car, into the bright sunshine. She still couldn't imagine that Sam wanted to play football, or that his grades were good enough if he did. Still, maybe it would bring the family together. She could imagine them all sitting in the bleachers, cheering for Sam's games.

Charlotte placed the box on the hood of her car and opened the backdoor. Rosemary would come to the games too. What was she thinking? Rosemary had never stopped going to the Bedford High football games, not for the last nearly fifty years, and she never missed a Cornhuskers game on TV either.

Toby trotted over to the car, begging to get in. "Not today." The dog whimpered. Charlotte slammed the back door and climbed into the driver's seat.

CHARLOTTE PARKED by the old shed at the far end of the home quarter. Bob pulled the pickup alongside her car and Pete bounded out, quickly climbing into the backseat.

Bob took his time climbing into the passenger seat, then picked at his lunch.

"What's the matter?" Charlotte asked.

"Just tired, is all. The roast is delicious, even better today than yesterday."

All the doors were open, letting in the fresh air and the flies and the musty smell of the stalks of corn to the right of the car.

Charlotte refilled Bob's coffee cup and handed it to him. "Maybe this will help perk you up." His face was flushed, but it *was* warm outside, and he had been working hard.

"We could use another driver." Pete held a cookie in each hand. "As soon as this afternoon."

"Hold your horses." Bob's hand shook a little as he clutched the coffee cup. "We're doing okay."

"No, we're getting behind. You keep taking too many breaks," Pete said. "How about Sam?"

"Not until his grades are up. Driving is a privilege he has to earn." Bob paused. "Besides, he doesn't have any experience."

"I was driving the trucks by the time I was thirteen," Pete insisted.

Charlotte shook her head.

"Well, Sam didn't grow up around farming the way you and Bill did. It's different." Bob paused again. "And besides, when your grades got bad, I shouldn't have let you drive either."

Charlotte glanced in the rearview mirror. Pete was frowning. "It wouldn't matter anyway," she said. "He's staying late after school tonight."

"Is the boy in trouble?" Bob asked.

Charlotte shook her head. "Coach Williams asked him to go to football practice today. The kicker—"

"Brendan Jackson," Pete chimed in.

"Yes. He broke his foot."

Pete clapped his hands together. "The kid wasn't any good anyways."

"Pete."

Bob's eyes lit up. "Sam's going to kick?"

"No. I mean, I don't know. Coach just wanted him to go to today's practice. That's all."

"I can't imagine Sam agreeing to play football even if Coach wants him," Pete said.

"Mom, can you drive the truck this afternoon?"

She shook her head. "Not today. I have to pick up Sam after practice."

"Then can you run into town for me? I got the wrong hose for the truck on Saturday."

"I can do it later this afternoon, when I pick up Sam."

Pete took out a pen and wrote what he needed on a scrap of paper. Then he climbed out of the car and slammed the door.

"Thanks," Bob muttered and then slammed his door.

She watched them walk to the pickup. Pete practically ran while Bob shuffled along, slowly limping. She needed to make sure and take a look at his leg that evening.

Charlotte drove back to the house and started working on finishing the dishes when the phone rang again. It was Hannah.

"How are things?" The cheerful voice of her neighbor and friend was music to her ears.

"All right." It was hard to explain over the phone.

Charlotte felt in the middle again. Emily's boy problem wasn't resolved, Christopher seemed troubled again, and who knew what would happen with Sam's mix of schoolwork and football? There was always something going on in a family, but surely she had learned that the first time around. It was foolish to anticipate anything else.

"Can you walk tonight?" Hannah asked.

Charlotte felt a rush of relief. "Yes," she said. That's what she needed, a long walk and chat with her friend. But if she walked tonight she wouldn't have time to pay the bills or be available to listen to Christopher if he was ready to talk. "I mean no, not tonight. How about tomorrow morning?"

Hannah sighed, and then agreed.

CHARLOTTE WALKED TOWARD the bus stop. She'd intended to start embroidering the kids' pillowcases this afternoon, but by the time she started the stew in the Crock-Pot and threw in a load of laundry, it was time for the kids to come home.

Toby stood at the end of the driveway, facing toward town, waiting for Christopher. When the dog started barking, Charlotte looked down the road, and a moment later the yellow bus, as bright as a crooked-neck squash, came into view.

Toby ran around in a circle, but stopped and sat down again by the time the bus stopped, waiting patiently for the kids to emerge.

A moment later, Christopher started down the stairs, a troubled look on his face.

"What's wrong?" Charlotte asked.

"Emily and Sam missed the bus." He shrugged. "Even though the driver waited."

"Sam stayed late. He called." Charlotte stepped back from the road with her arm around Christopher. But where was Emily? She and Christopher started toward the house with Toby nipping at their heels, barking a welcome.

Christopher ignored her. "What about Emily?"

"Maybe she stayed to get help with algebra," Charlotte said hopefully. Charlotte hurried her steps. Maybe Emily was calling for a ride right now.

Toby began barking again, and Christopher turned toward the road. "Look, Grandma."

Sean's black Mustang appeared, rounding the corner. Rayann waved out of the passenger window as they pulled into the driveway. "We have Emily with us. She missed the bus!" Rayann called.

Charlotte wasn't sure whether to be annoyed or relieved. At least Emily was safe, and she didn't have to squeeze in a trip into town before going back to get the hose and pick up Sam. Sean pulled behind Charlotte's car and turned the engine off. He and his sister climbed out of the car.

Emily crawled out of the backseat, wearing Rayann's Cornhuskers sweatshirt. "I'm sorry, Grandma. Honestly. I didn't do it on purpose. Ashley borrowed my jacket this morning and I couldn't find her after school, which was a little annoying. Then the bus had already left and Rayann said they could give me a ride, to save you a trip."

Charlotte realized her arms were crossed and let them drop by her side.

"I tried to call on my cell, but the battery was dead." Emily slung her book bag over her shoulder. "I'm really sorry."

"And our cells aren't working!" Rayann said. "Otherwise she would have called."

"You have a nice place." Sean said, looking around from the fields to the barn to the house. He seemed oblivious to the girls' apologies.

"Thank you," Charlotte said. She took a deep breath. "And thank you for giving Emily a ride, although, Emily, you should have gone back to the office and called."

"I know I should have, but it would have taken longer." She turned toward Rayann and Sean. "Do you guys want to come in and get a snack?"

Oh dear. Charlotte crossed her arms again. "Not today, sweetie. I need to go into town and run some errands before I pick up Sam."

Emily flipped her hair over her shoulder. "Can't they just come in for a snack?"

"We don't have time to stay anyway." Sean tossed his keys in the air. "We need to get home."

"But thank you." Rayann gave Emily a quick hug.

As Sean drove away, Emily muttered, "Yeah, thanks" under her breath, directing her comment toward Charlotte.

"Emily, it wouldn't have worked to have them stay."

"Why don't you trust me?"

Christopher slipped between Charlotte and Emily and into the house.

Emily pressed her lips together and spoke quietly. "Mom always said you were strict."

TWO HOURS LATER Charlotte pulled up alongside the football field next to the high school. There was a group of players on the field running through an obstacle course of tires, and a second group running around the track. Was Sam out there?

She climbed out of the car and stood beside the chain-link fence. All of the players looked alike in their blue practice jerseys, except for Sam. He wore soccer shorts, a white T-shirt, and sneakers. He stood on the thirty-yard line. The coach held his hand up and Sam ran forward, sending the ball sailing through the sky, easily through the goal posts.

The coach blew his whistle, and the players gathered in the middle of the field. A boy on crutches lagged behind. A few minutes later Sam ran toward her, swinging his backpack.

"How did it go?" Charlotte asked as she climbed into the car.

"Okay. I would have done better if I had my cleats, but I'll bring them tomorrow." Sam sat down in the passenger seat and slammed the door.

"How did Brendan break his leg?"

"Motocross accident on Saturday. Coach was really ticked." Sam shifted in his seat. "I wish you'd let me drive. How am I ever going to get my license if I can't practice?"

"One of these days." Charlotte smiled at her grandson. Though Sam had his learner's permit, she was always nervous when he got behind the wheel, regardless of his grades. Charlotte raised an eyebrow and put the car into gear. "Well, I guess if Coach puts you on the team we'll soon know how your grades are. Right?"

Sam sighed.

Charlotte waited a long moment and then asked, "How was school today? Besides football."

Sam shrugged. "I got a C on that English essay that I redid.

Miss Simons said I would have had an A if I'd done it right the first time."

Charlotte bit her tongue to keep herself from lecturing him.

"How's Emily?" Sam asked.

"Fine." Charlotte opened her window an inch, welcoming the fresh air. What did Sam know?

"Did you see who she got a ride home with?"

Charlotte nodded. "She missed the bus."

"Not really." Sam laughed. "She was stalling."

Charlotte kept her eyes on the road.

"Emily practically stalks him at school. She walks by his locker between every class."

"Sam."

"It's true. She had a major crush on my friend Jordan back in California, and that's what she did then too." Sam rolled down his window a little. "Emily is right, though. He did break up with his girlfriend. At least that's what he said." Sam tapped the air-freshener tree hanging from the rearview mirror. "There's one thing that's really cool about Sean, though. His car. He's really lucky."

"It's a nice car."

"Mom and I had talked about me getting a car by the time I was a senior. She said I could bus tables at the restaurant when I wasn't playing soccer. She was probably going to get promoted to manager."

Charlotte didn't answer. The restaurant where Denise worked was very nice and attracted lots of tourists; Sam would have done well busing tables there.

"Maybe I can get a job soon and start saving money for a car."

Charlotte nodded. "That's a good idea." Bill had driven one of the farm pickups when he was younger, and Denise had often used Charlotte's car, an old Buick back then. Pete had inherited Lazarus all those years ago, and even then the truck had been ancient. Did kids nowadays expect to drive Mustangs? She and Bob couldn't afford to help Sam get a nice car like that, and even if they could they wouldn't.

"Are you tired, Grandma?"

She smiled. "Just a little." She was getting a headache.

"I could drive."

Charlotte glanced at him and just shook her head.

Toby and Christopher ran to meet them as Charlotte pulled into the driveway.

"How are things?" she asked, stepping onto the gravel.

"Fine. I finished my homework. Toby helped. And I set the table."

"Thank you. Where's Emily?"

"In her room, talking on the phone."

Sam strode into the house, and Christopher took off behind the shed with Toby. Charlotte hung up her jacket and washed her hands at the kitchen sink. The table was set with the forks, knives, and spoons placed haphazardly around the plates. The glasses were on the left-hand side and the napkins were in a stack in the middle of the table.

She started up the stairs and saw Sam standing at Emily's door, leaning in.

"You were stalling. I watched you."

"I forgot my algebra book and had to go back to my locker." Emily's voice sounded a bit defensive.

"Yeah, right."

"And then, get this."

Charlotte stopped midway up the stairs.

"When I got here, with Rayann and Sean, Grandma wouldn't let them in the house because she had to go into town. She's unbelievably strict. It's embarrassing." Emily's voice rose.

"So? I wouldn't have let them in the house either."

"You're full of it. Remember back home? We had friends over all the time."

"Well, most of the time Mom didn't know."

"What's with you?"

"Nothing."

"Is it football? Now you fit in so you're going to be all—"

"Sam. Emily." Charlotte hurried up the rest of the stairs.

"It's not football. I don't even know if Coach wants me, and I don't even know if I want to play."

"Yeah, right."

"You two, stop. Now." Charlotte wedged her way between them.

Emily retreated into her room and slammed the door.

"Sam, get your shower. Then both of you come help get dinner on the table."

Charlotte started back down the steps and then spun around, back to Emily's room. She knocked.

Emily flung the door open. "Oh. It's you."

"You told me you went back for your jacket because Ashley had it."

"Pardon?" Emily stepped backward into her room and sat on the bed.

"Which did you go back for after school? Your jacket or your algebra book?"

Emily hesitated and then answered, "Both. I forgot my book in my locker, and I had to find Ashley before she left."

"Oh." Charlotte turned. She wasn't sure she believed her, but what had she expected Emily to say? "Come down and help with dinner, please," she said over her shoulder.

Charlotte took two ibuprofen tablets for her headache and then pulled a bag of rolls from the pantry, dumping them into the bread basket. She searched the vegetable drawer and pulled out carrots, a stalk of celery, and two cucumbers. She would make a vegetable plate. She microwaved a cup of cold coffee, hoping the caffeine would help her feel better.

She wanted Emily to be honest, more than anything. The only thing she had ever spanked her children for was lying, Pete the most and Denise a couple of times. She didn't remember ever spanking Bill. But who knew? Maybe he just didn't get caught.

A vehicle pulled into the driveway. *It's 6:30 already?*

Pete stormed through the backdoor; Bob followed at a slower pace.

"Dinner's not quite ready." Charlotte sipped the coffee, burning her tongue.

"We wanted to get back out to the field." Pete kicked his boots off and one slid halfway across the kitchen floor. "We have a small patch left to do tonight."

Christopher slammed through the door. "Grandma! Toby's limping!"

Sam's footsteps thundered down the stairs, followed by Emily's lighter steps.

"I told you to stay out of it." Emily's voice grew louder as she stalked after Sam. "You're full of it, Sam!"

"Charlotte, you said to come in at six thirty." Bob pulled his work gloves from his hands.

She put her cup on the counter, splashing coffee onto

the Formica, and faced the crowd of needy people in front of her. Everyone was talking at once. She paused for a moment and then fled out the back door.

"What's wrong with Grandma?" she heard Emily ask just as the door flapped shut behind her.

Pete said something, but Charlotte couldn't make out his words.

They were probably a perfectly normal family under the circumstances, but she'd had enough for the moment. They weren't one of those sitcom families on TV that Hannah liked so much. Charlotte couldn't come up with a one-liner that would make everyone laugh and get along.

She stopped in the middle of the yard. Geese honked faintly in the distance, and she headed toward the creek, breathing in the cool evening air. Her head throbbed. She stopped at the banks of the creek. Below, a mother duck and her nearly grown ducklings skirted across the water toward the overhang of willow branches. "Dear God," she prayed, "I'm tired."

Charlotte had needed some downtime today, and hadn't gotten any. She needed to take time for herself, to embroider, to read, to study her Bible. A walk with Hannah in the morning would do her good.

The geese honked again.

"They're around the bend." She turned her head. Christopher was standing behind her. He must have followed her. "Toby chased them away earlier. That's when she started limping, but the geese came back."

"Did you come down here while I was gone?" Charlotte narrowed her eyes at him. Christopher knew he was strictly forbidden to come to the creek alone.

He shook his head. "I stood in the field and yelled at Toby."

Charlotte patted his shoulder. "I'll take a look at Toby now. Let's go up by the shop." They stopped under the light, and Charlotte checked the dog's right paw. A thorn was buried halfway in the pad. She grasped it between her thumb and index finger and pulled it out.

"Is she okay?" Christopher asked.

"She's fine." Charlotte held out the paw for him to see. "It was just a thorn. Next time you can check and pull it out."

"I'm sorry." Christopher shoved his hands in his pocket.

"Why are you sorry?" Charlotte stood.

"That you're mad."

"I'm not mad. Just overwhelmed." She put her arm around Christopher. "And I'm the one who's sorry. I shouldn't have stormed out like that."

"No. That was okay, Grandma. You needed a time-out and you took one."

She laughed.

"That's what Mom used to tell me to do. To take a time-out, on my own, before she had to give me one."

"I like that. Thank you, Christopher," Charlotte said, then turned toward the house to face the others.

Chapter Twelve

"I brought you a chocolate-mint cake," Hannah announced, coming through the back door after a quick knock and a yoo-hoo.

Charlotte stood with her hat on, ready to walk. She took the sheet pan from her friend. "It smells delicious. Thank you! Let's each have a piece after our walk, with our coffee."

Toby met them outside the door, wagging her tail.

"Let's go, girl." Hannah led the way toward the trail along the creek. They chatted for a few minutes, and then Charlotte broached the subject that had been bugging her since the day before. "Do you think that I'm too strict?"

"Who says you're strict?"

"Emily." Charlotte quickened her pace to match Hannah's longer, and younger, stride.

"All kids think their parents are strict, or in your case, grandparents. It's part of life." Hannah turned onto the trail. "You probably wouldn't be doing your job if she didn't think you were strict." A slight breeze rustled through the weeping willow branches. The creek ran low, but still Charlotte could make out a trout swimming in the middle. It jumped and snatched at something on the surface of the water.

"It's hard to figure this out." Charlotte slipped her hat off her head and clutched it in her hand. The morning was warming.

"Well, you did fine the first time around. Pete's come along, and look at the great job Denise did with Sam, Emily, and Christopher, all on her own." Hannah stepped ahead on the narrow path. Toby zipped by both of them.

Denise *had* done a good job with her kids. It was obvious how much she had loved them and how much the kids had loved her.

Hannah took off her knit hat and ran her hand through her graying blonde hair. "All families have their problems, Charlotte. Remember the *Brady Bunch* episode when the other kids caught Greg smoking and Marcia told on him? I was so surprised that the Bradys would have to deal with something like that!"

Charlotte laughed. No, she didn't remember that episode, but leave it to Hannah to remember a TV show that had aired decades ago. Denise used to watch the reruns after school, and they were fifteen years old then. "Thanks, Hannah. What did I do to deserve a friend like you?"

Hannah waved both of her hands from side to side. "Maybe God knew that the Stevenson family needed two women to pray. That's why he matched us up." Hannah continued, "Besides, they've added so much to my life. *The Brady Bunch* and *The Cosby Show* and *The Facts of Life* have all been entertaining, but your family is real. I've learned a lot."

They crossed the creek on the age-old wooden bridge and turned up to the road. Toby barked as they walked around the curve in the road, against the traffic. "Well, if you're not tired of me complaining, let me tell you about last night." Charlotte told Hannah about feeling overwhelmed and rushing out into the backyard, but she didn't go into detail about what Sam and Emily were arguing about or Bob being upset that dinner was late. "I felt like a fool." Her face warmed.

"And how did the rest of the evening go after that?"

"Fine. Everyone was nice." Charlotte sighed. "The kids didn't bicker. Sam and Emily cleaned up after dinner without me asking."

Hannah laughed. "Sounds like it did them good to have you reach your limit."

A truck rumbled toward them. Charlotte recognized it as Bob's, piled high with a full load. He leaned forward against the steering wheel. Charlotte waved.

"Is he all right?" Hannah asked.

"I don't know." Charlotte stopped. The truck slowed. Charlotte waved both hands at Bob. He waved back. "Stop!" she yelled. Something was wrong. Toby ran ahead, barking. The truck rolled onto the gravel.

Bob opened his window. "What's wrong?" he asked.

"You were driving all hunched over." Charlotte jogged toward him.

"My leg hurts. I was just rubbing it."

"Bob."

He shrugged. "I'm fine, Charlotte."

"You're not fine. You were practically driving off the road. Let me look at your leg."

He shook his head.

"Come on. Put your foot on the bumper, so I can check out your bruise."

He shook his head again.

"Bob, I'm not moving until you show me. I should have checked it sooner."

He opened the truck door and slowly stepped down. His leg gave way and he grabbed the door handle.

"I'm fine," he said with a grimace on his face.

"You're not fine." She kneeled down to the ground and lifted the pants leg of Bob's coveralls. A nasty purple bruise covered his leg. There was a hard lump in the center.

"I think we should have you go see the doctor." She ran her fingers over the bruise lightly.

"It's just a bruise." Bob swatted her hand away and stepped back into the cab. "And besides, we're already behind with harvest."

"I'll go call the doctor and see if we can get you in right away while you take this load to the elevator."

Bob shook his head.

"Bob." Hannah stepped forward. "Do you remember that school superintendent a few years ago? The one who died from a blood clot?"

A puzzled expression spread over Bob's face.

"Bob, you went on that call with the volunteer firefighters." Charlotte put her hands on her hips.

He nodded. "But that's not what this is." Bob's voice was growing more frustrated.

"He was dead, just like that." Hannah snapped her fingers.

"Bob, let's just have the doctor take a look at it." Charlotte stepped closer to her husband. "We have these kids to take care of. I don't want anything to happen to you. With your condition, we can't take any chances." Bob didn't like to be reminded of his diabetes, which meant Charlotte had to be even more vigilant.

Bob let out a long breath. "I'll stop by the house after I get rid of this load." He shifted the truck into drive. "Call and see what the doctor says."

"Okay." Charlotte nodded. "And stop rubbing your leg. We want to get you to the doctor in one piece."

CHARLOTTE STOOD at the clinic reception desk with the phone in her hand. What was Hannah's number? She'd been dialing it for the last thirty years. It took a moment until it came to her. She dialed quickly.

Hannah answered on the first ring. "They did an ultrasound on his leg," Charlotte said.

"Is it a blood clot?" Hannah asked. Charlotte could hear the low sound of a television playing behind her.

"They don't know yet."

"How's his blood sugar?"

"He's low so they gave him some glucose, but his blood pressure is high, 180/130."

"That's not good." Hannah's voice held even more concern. "Let me know what happens." Charlotte promised to keep her updated and hung up the phone to check on Bob.

Bob tried to sit up when Charlotte entered the examination room. "This is ridiculous," he said. "A calf kicked me in the leg. It's not a big deal."

Charlotte picked a *Parents* magazine from the rack and sat down in the one chair in the room. If he was grumpy, she'd just ignore him.

An hour later, a nurse's aide popped her head into the room and asked Bob if he was ready for lunch.

"It's too early for lunch."

"Bob, you need to eat." Charlotte stood and placed the magazine on the chair. The clock above the door read 11:45.

"You have plenty of time." The nurse placed a tray on the table beside the bed. "Dr. Carr got called out on an emergency. He said to tell you he'll be back as soon as he can."

Bob picked at the turkey sandwich on the tray and then ate the celery sticks and Jell-O. Charlotte ate the chips and then picked up the magazine again. Forty-five minutes later Dr. Carr billowed through the curtain.

"What you have is a blood clot, Bob, a deep-vein thrombosis," he said, his forehead wrinkled. "It's a good thing you came in."

Charlotte stood and stepped close to her husband. He sat up slowly, his gray hair smashed against the side of his head. "You're kidding." Bob's grumpiness vanished.

Dr. Carr continued, "We'll start you on Heparin. It's a blood thinner."

Bob nodded.

"And you need to take it easy for a couple of days. No working." The doctor chuckled. "Remember, you *are* sixty-five. And no sitting in one place too long; get up and move around every hour and take short walks."

Charlotte put her hand on Bob's shoulder.

"Then we'll take another blood test on Friday, and if that's good we'll start you on a different blood thinner for a few weeks."

"What about his blood pressure?" Charlotte asked.

Dr. Carr stuck his hand into the pocket of his lab coat. "It's definitely high." He took out his pad and pen.

"More meds." Bob exhaled slowly.

Dr. Carr handed the prescription to Bob, who passed it on to Charlotte.

"We'll give you the Heparin intravenously, so you'll need to spend the night."

"Spend the night?" Bob's face reddened.

Dr. Carr raised his eyebrows. "Sorry, Bob. I get to call the shots on this one."

Charlotte stopped by the nurses' station and called Hannah again as the orderly moved Bob to a hospital room. Charlotte asked her friend to go tell Pete and then to call Bill, Rosemary, and Pastor Nathan.

Thirty minutes later, Bob was wearing a gown and the nurse had started his IV. Charlotte folded his clothes and put them in the closet as he talked with Bill on the phone.

There was a half knock on the door as Pete barged in. "Dad, are you all right?"

"Gotta go," Bob said to Bill. He hung up the phone and shifted his head from behind the IV pole so he could see Pete. "You won't be getting the farm anytime soon."

"Bob." Charlotte hugged Pete. "He's as ornery as ever."

"Hannah said it's a blood clot."

"Yep." Bob reached down and patted his leg. "Deep-vein thrombosis."

"What?"

"A blood clot," Charlotte explained. "From getting kicked by the calf."

"Don't people die from blood clots?" Pete asked.

"Not me," Bob answered. "Not this time."

Charlotte sank down into the well-worn chair by the bed, feeling absolutely spent.

"Who's going to help me with harvest?" Pete asked.

"Let's talk about this later." Charlotte stretched out her legs.

"I'll be out of here tomorrow," Bob said.

"Did you listen to Dr. Carr? You can't drive the truck for at least a few days." Charlotte stood. "So, we'll talk about harvest later." She gave Pete her most intense *mom* look. She didn't care if he was a grown-up.

Pete sulked, and ten minutes later left to get back to work.

"Could you hand me my hat?" Bob asked Charlotte.

"Pardon?"

He never wore his hat in buildings. He was old-fashioned about that.

"Just hand me my hat. I feel naked in this gown." He still looked pale and his hair was all askew.

Charlotte laughed and complied and then sat down on the edge of the bed.

"Did I scare you?" Bob squeezed Charlotte's hand.

Charlotte nodded. "A little."

"Ahh." Melody stood in the doorway wearing her red *Mel's Place* apron with a smudge of flour on it. "It just gets sweeter, doesn't it?" Melody pushed the IV pole back a little. "Rosemary called and told me, and I came as soon as my lunch rush was over."

"Thanks," Charlotte said. Bob nodded.

"I can take Sam home after football practice if that will help. It's no bother," Melody said. "And Charlotte, I'm bringing sandwiches for you and the kids, a tofu salad one for Emily, and minestrone soup."

"You don't need to do that," Charlotte said.

"No, I do. And if you don't need it, that's fine, but I need to do it."

Charlotte gave her a weak smile. "Actually, I do need it."

"Good." Melody nodded. "Then I'm helping both of us."

"Thank you, Melody."

"So when do you get out of here?" Melody asked, reaching for Bob's hand.

"Tomorrow morning."

"Sounds like it's for the best. Seems like someone was watching over you."

Bob nodded and glanced at Charlotte.

"Rosemary said she was heading up here in a few minutes."

"Oh, good." Charlotte stood. Bob wouldn't be alone after she left to meet the bus. If she headed home now she'd have time to fix a snack for the kids.

Melody stood too. "I've got to buzz, but you two make sure and let me know what else I can do, you hear?"

Bob thanked her, and Charlotte bent to kiss her husband. "I'll be back this evening, maybe with the kids."

"Don't make them come if they don't want too," he said. "I'd rather they not see me like this."

Chapter Thirteen

"So Grandpa's going to be okay?" Christopher said, swinging his backpack onto a chair.

Charlotte nodded as she started a pot of coffee. "Just fine. He's on medicine that will make the blood clot dissolve, like a lump of sugar in water."

Emily picked up an apple from the fruit bowl. "How long will he be in the hospital?"

Charlotte poured Christopher a glass of milk. "Just overnight."

"I don't really like hospitals," Christopher said quietly and then turned back to his homework. Emily nodded, books spread out on the table in front of her. The children were quiet as they did their homework.

"Christopher, how's your report coming along?" Charlotte asked as she put a plate of cookies on the table.

"Fine." He grabbed a few cookies and stood and gathered his book and papers. "I'm going to go outside to work, so Toby can help me." A few minutes later Pete parked the truck beside the house.

"Grandma," Christopher yelled from the front porch. "Can I ride to the grain elevator with Pete?"

Charlotte said yes and then sank into her chair, exhausted. She had intended to do housework today and catch up on the laundry. She rocked slowly, back and forth, sipping her coffee. What if Bob hadn't agreed to go to the clinic? What if she and Hannah hadn't been walking this morning? What if Bob hadn't been rubbing his leg?

So many what ifs. Life was so fragile. Denise rolled her car; Bob got to the clinic on time. Who could guess at what God might allow to happen?

Charlotte shivered. He was in control. That was all that she could cling to.

An hour later, Pete and Christopher came through the back door with Sam, carrying bags of food from Melody. "She said she'd call in the morning to see how Grandpa is." Sam said, slinging the bag of sandwiches onto the table.

As they sat down to eat, after Charlotte prayed and thanked God that Bob was all right, Pete said that they needed a second driver. "We needed someone before all of this happened with Dad, but now we really do."

Charlotte frowned.

"I could drive the truck after school," Sam said.

Charlotte shook her head.

"Grandma, why not?"

"Your grades," she answered.

"Football," Pete said.

"I couldn't care less about football." Sam pushed his chair away from the table.

"Football is irrelevant," Charlotte said. "Grandpa told you your grades need to be better."

Sam's face hardened. Charlotte felt for her grandson, but

she had no words to comfort him. The driving issue was up to him, although perhaps a blessing in disguise. Having Sam not drive gave Charlotte one less thing to worry about.

"That doesn't solve our problem until Dad can drive again." Pete helped himself to more soup.

"I can drive tomorrow," Charlotte said. "After I pick up Dad and get him settled."

Pete grunted.

"I'll drive the next day too." Charlotte took a bite of the sandwich. She hoped Bob would be okay to stay by himself and follow the doctor's orders without her being around to enforce them.

The family ate in silence.

THE NEXT MORNING, after the kids had raced out to the bus, Charlotte finished up the dishes and headed to her car. The cows gathered around the gate and mooed, and the calves kicked up their hooves by the far fence. It had been two days now since an escape. Toby barked from the lawn.

Bob was dressed and waiting in the chair of his hospital room with his hat in his lap when Charlotte arrived. "What took you so long?" he asked.

Charlotte picked up his jacket and helped him to his feet.

"Here are the prescriptions." Bob handed her three slips of paper.

They walked slowly down the hall. "Maybe we should pull out your dad's old cane," Charlotte said. "I think it's still in the attic."

"Maybe we shouldn't." Bob speeded up a little.

An hour later, after a long wait at the pharmacy, Bob sank into his chair in the family room, his medications lined up in a pillbox on the end table. Charlotte put a glass of water with a straw next to the box. "Are you sure you're okay with me leaving you alone?" she asked as she pulled her jacket off the hooks by the door.

"I'd be better if you'd just let me drive." Bob pushed back in his recliner. "Doctors say things all the time that they don't mean. Me driving from here to the elevator and back isn't any different than me sitting in this dad-gum chair all day."

Charlotte shook her head.

"Well, don't sit all day. Make sure and get up and walk around every hour or so." Charlotte tried to sound chipper. "I'll be back at lunch time."

Bob grunted.

CHARLOTTE DROVE DOWN to the home quarter. Pete said they had one last patch to finish up before moving on to the next field. She pulled the grain truck up beside the combine for an on-the-go load. Pete swung the auger over the bed of the truck. Pete's music blared; Charlotte concentrated on staying even with the combine as she glanced Pete's way every few seconds. The corn pouring into the back of the truck sent a steady vibration through the cab. She wished Pete would turn down the music; she couldn't make out the song, but all the commotion was making her nervous.

Pete signaled to her that the truck was full, and she pulled away toward the road and then turned left, heading to the grain elevators. They stood like concrete giants in the distance, three behemoth cylinders guarding the prairie, guarding their livelihood. Fortunately for the Stevensons, the elevators were just three miles from the farm.

Charlotte pulled into the elevator yard, and the foreman, Lewis Bell, pointed her to the scales. He weighed the load and then took a sample of the grain to test for moisture, weight, and debris, and then directed her to back up. She positioned the truck over the grate, hoisted the bed, and released the end gate. As the grain poured through the back of the truck and into the underground bin, she rolled down her window and then wiggled out of her jacket.

"I heard that grandson of yours is going to play football," Lewis said.

"Maybe," Charlotte answered, studying him. Lewis had been a year or two behind Pete in high school. He had played football, basketball, and baseball. He'd left Bedford for college but then returned a year or two ago.

"A little late in the season, isn't it? Especially for a kid who's never played before?"

Charlotte tried to smile. "We'll see." She returned the clipboard.

A few minutes later, after the empty truck had been weighed and Lewis had given her a receipt, she was back on the road, headed to the farm, and listening to the farm report on the radio. The price of corn was still going up. She shifted into second and crossed into the field. Charlotte positioned the truck alongside the combine again. Far in the distance, she could hear Toby bark, probably at the geese that were just settling along the creek.

She sank back against the seat, thankful for her life,

thankful that Bob was all right. Pete swung the auger over again and started loading. She thought of her grandparents and the thresher they had used. She never saw it in action; it had been long retired behind their old barn by the time she came along, but she used to play on it as a child, clambering up onto the rusted seat, imagining eight horses pulling the contraption. Her grandfather would be dismayed at the cab Pete sat in. It was like an office on wheels, with an air conditioner, radio, CD player, outside thermometer, and moisture gauge.

Sam, Emily, and Christopher had no idea how quickly their lives would fly by, and that was why she wanted, desperately, for them to get the training they needed now, and why she would do anything she could to make sure they stayed on track.

Train up a child in the way he should go: and when he is old, he will not depart from it. The familiar proverb used to haunt her after Denise left and during Pete's teenage years. *When a child is* old *he will not depart from it*. She almost burst into laughter. *Old!* Why hadn't she registered that word before? Denise never had the chance to become old, but Charlotte could see that she had been returning to her training in the way she disciplined her kids and in the way she had talked to them about God, even though she didn't take them to church.

Old. Maybe there was still hope for Pete. After all, he had gone to church a few times in the last little while. Maybe he went for the sake of the kids. Maybe he went to catch a glimpse of Dana. Maybe he went for his own sake. She wasn't going to try to guess at what motivated Pete.

She definitely had more patience for parenting the

second time around. Life didn't seem as urgent. It wasn't that it didn't feel frantic with everything that needed to be done, but still, she felt there was more time for the children to learn from their mistakes, from their choices, than she had before.

Pete waved that the truck was full. She was trying to let Sam figure out his schoolwork, to not get over involved, not the way she had when Pete was in high school. She pulled away and bounced across the field toward the road.

Charlotte frowned. But Emily and boys was a different matter. She had no patience for that. The consequences were too permanent.

She turned onto the highway. Driving the truck for a day or two was a nice change of pace, but she couldn't keep it up through all of the harvest. She would ask Melody if she knew of someone who could use a little extra cash. Or maybe Pastor Nathan might have an idea.

Charlotte turned onto the highway. One more load to the elevator and then it would be time to hurry back to the house to get lunch on the table and to check on Bob.

Chapter Fourteen

Emily stood at the entrance of the cafeteria holding her lunch bag. She had yogurt, an apple, and a bag of almonds, and the peanut butter sandwich Grandma made her every morning that she never ate. She wasn't sure about the peanut butter; it wasn't organic, and it tasted too sweet and creamy, like corn syrup and shortening had been added.

She headed toward the front of the line and excused herself as she grabbed a metal spoon. In San Diego the cafeteria had sporks, plastic spoons with tines. Ashley sat in the middle of the room where they always sat. She waved. Emily waved back and headed toward her, settling down across the table from her. Then Emily scanned the room again. A group of students surged in, including Rayann, who took a place in the hot-lunch line. She wore Hollister jeans and a tank top with a gauzy shirt over it, and her hair was straightened. She was the prettiest girl in the room.

Emily didn't see Sean anywhere. She should have stalled and waited for Rayann. Last Friday Sean had been late for lunch but sat by Rayann. Emily had sat by Ashley that day too. Tomorrow she would take her time at her locker and maybe stop at the water fountain again before heading to the cafeteria.

"How's your grandpa doing?" Ashley asked as she flicked a crumb off the sleeve of her red blouse.

"Fine." Emily opened her lunch bag. "He's fine. He's getting out of the hospital today." At least that was the plan.

"Mom said it's really a blessing that he's okay." Ashley's voice oozed with compassion. "We prayed for him last night."

"Oh." Emily shrugged and then added, "We prayed for him too." At least Grandma had at dinner, and she probably had again when she tucked Christopher into bed. "That was really nice of your mom to drop off dinner."

Ashley smiled. "She really likes to do that sort of thing."

Emily nodded. Somehow that made it sound like it wasn't that special, wasn't just for her family. It sounded like Melody did that sort of thing all the time.

"Your grandpa probably won't be running after calves anymore," Ashley said in all seriousness. "Boy, between his diabetes, high blood pressure, and blood clot, he'd really better take easy."

Emily didn't even try to smile. What did running after calves have to do with his blood clot? And why did Ashley seem to know more about Grandpa's health than she did?

Emily looked toward the end of the line again. Still no Sean. She didn't want to talk about Grandpa with Ashley.

Sam appeared with his lunch and headed toward Emily. She wrinkled her nose. He had a beef enchilada on his plate with extra shredded meat piled on top. "Don't worry," he said, "I'm not sitting by you. I'm just getting close enough to scare you." He tipped his tray toward her and laughed.

Ashley waved at Sam; he nodded and kept walking toward a football player at the far table.

The night before Mom had her accident, Emily had been bugging her to go the mall. She complained that Mom drove Sam places all the time—to soccer practice, to soccer games, to soccer tournaments. All Emily wanted to do was go to the mall and shop at Forever 21. Mom said she was too tired, so Emily pouted. Mom said that the way Emily was acting was making her exhausted, and Emily yelled at Mom, saying that she never did anything for her, only Sam.

Maybe that was why Mom wrecked the car the next day, because she was so tired, because Emily had made her tired.

Had she been being nice to Grandpa lately? Was Grandpa going to be okay?

"I'm sure your grandpa will be fine." Ashley's eyes were so sweet and kind that Emily had to bite her lip to keep from screaming.

"Listen, Ashley," she said. "I don't want to talk about Grandpa, okay? Just can it."

Ashley blinked her eyes quickly as her face reddened almost to the same color of her blouse.

"Hi. Am I interrupting?" Rayann came up behind Emily.

"No," Ashley answered quietly.

Rayann sat down, a big smile plastered across her face.

"I can see why you always bring your lunch." Rayann speared a piece of brown lettuce with her fork. "My high school in Lincoln, the one I started at this year for all of five weeks, has off-campus lunch with a dozen fast food places within a couple of blocks."

Emily wrinkled her nose. *Yuck.*

"Not your thing?" Rayann laughed. "Well, fast food is

better than these school lunches and a whole lot better than any of the restaurants in Bedford."

Ashley pushed her hair away from her face and in an amazingly composed voice said, "Like Mel's Place?"

"Exactly!" Rayann pointed her finger toward her open mouth, making a gag-me gesture.

Ashley just stared at Rayann.

"Rayann." Emily laughed, nervously. She was a little surprised at Ashley for baiting her. Maybe Ashley had more spunk than Emily had thought.

"What?" Rayann asked.

"My mom is Mel, and I work there sometimes." Ashley's eyebrows stayed arched as her gaze never left Rayann's face.

Rayann rolled her eyes. "Great. So basically, I just put both feet in my mouth?"

"Basically," Ashley answered.

Rayann giggled. "Oh! Awkward! I take it all back. Mel's is great. I especially love the espresso macchiatos there. Best I've ever had."

Emily smiled awkwardly.

Ashley didn't look amused. "There's your brother," she said to Rayann, pointing across the cafeteria.

Emily couldn't help from turning her head. Sean wore a black sweater and stood in the middle of the double doorway talking to Miss Simons.

"*Ooh*. Looks like he's in trouble." Rayann picked up her fork again. "Miss Simons is *so* mean."

Ashley shook her head. "No, she's really nice."

"I know." Rayann smiled. "I was just kidding."

Ashley tossed her hair over her shoulder as if she'd had

enough. "Didn't your uncle used to date Miss Simons, Emily?" Ashley asked.

"Not really." Emily shook her head slightly. What was Ashley doing? Emily hated small towns, Bedford in particular.

Rayann turned toward Emily, amused, and then said, "I think Mr. Santos likes her." She speared an anemic cherry tomato and held it up.

"Well, at least Mr. Santos graduated from college. And high school," Ashley said.

A lump formed in Emily's throat. What was going on with Ashley?

"What? Your uncle didn't graduate?" Rayann tilted her head to the side. "But he got his GED, right?"

Emily shook her head again.

"That's weird." Rayann put her fork down and took a sip of her milk. She made a face. "I think it's sour. Ewww."

"Mine was fine," Ashley said.

Rayann ignored her. "So, why *would* Miss Simons ever come back to Bedford?"

"I heard she really missed it," Ashley said. "That she really wanted to come back."

Rayann's eyes grew large. "Hard to imagine."

Across the room, Sean smiled at Miss Simons and then walked out of the cafeteria.

"Earth to Emily," Ashley said as she stood. "Remember? Earth. Nebraska. Bedford. Heather Creek Farm. Your horses." Ashley paused. Emily just stared at her.

"Never mind." Ashley picked up her tray.

"Good grief." Rayann snickered. "What's with her?"

Chapter Fifteen

Charlotte pulled into the driveway. A breeze swayed the branches of the maple tree, spreading more leaves across the lawn; she would ask Christopher to rake after school.

She petted Toby and inhaled the pungent scent of burning leaves. A veil of smoke rose in the distance over the Carter place. Hannah was ahead of her in getting her autumn chores done. Charlotte headed into the kitchen and put leftover stew on the stove to heat for lunch.

She heard Pete's voice in the family room and assumed he was talking to Bob.

"Okay, I'll expect his call." Pete's voice sounded a little formal. What was going on?

Charlotte rounded the corner into the family room.

"Thank you. I really appreciate your help." Pete sat at the desk and held the phone against his ear.

"Okay, then. See you around. Bye, Dana."

Dana! "Pete?" Charlotte said.

He spun around.

"Who were you talking to?"

He put the phone on the desk. "I was just making a few phone calls about hiring a driver."

"And?"

"I've been asking around, and I think I have a lead." Pete stood. "I need to get washed up for lunch."

Charlotte tilted her head. "Where's Dad?"

"Out on the porch, pacing."

Charlotte opened the front door and greeted Bob. "How do you feel?"

"Like I'm tired of everyone asking me how I feel." He stepped toward the door.

"Did you know that Pete's looking for a driver?"

"He told me. I told him not to bother. I'm going to be fine soon enough."

"I don't know. Maybe we should have someone, at least part-time, no matter what." It would take the pressure off Bob. Pete was anxious to make up for the lost time, and if Bob needed to rest more in the next couple of weeks, a part-time driver would allow that.

Bob followed her into the kitchen silently. Charlotte turned the stew to low. What was Pete up to?

"How long can you drive this afternoon?" Pete asked as they sat down at the table.

"Until I go get Sam. Emily will have to put dinner together, I guess."

"Great." Pete slumped into a chair. "Tofu burgers."

The phone rang just as Bob finished saying the blessing. Charlotte excused herself and got up to answer it.

It was Bill. "I have the girls with me, there's an in-service day at their school, and we're going to be out your way later this afternoon. I need to take a look at a piece of property in Monroe County that's in probate. Anna has her book group tonight, so she suggested that we eat with you."

Six months ago, she lived for visits from Bill and the girls. Today, it felt like a little too much to add to the mix.

"Oh."

"We'll see you around five then."

"Bill, I'm driving truck for Pete and Dad. Could you pick up Sam for me in town? At football practice." She would have to stop helping with the harvest early if she was going to make dinner. Pete wouldn't understand, but she *was* compromising.

"Football! Since when?"

After explaining what was going on with Sam, she hung up. She could have asked him to drive truck while she went into town, except she couldn't imagine Bill driving the truck, wearing his suit and tie, and besides, he had never liked it, not even when he was in high school and college. Anyway, she would still need to fix dinner.

"Bill and the girls are coming for dinner," she said as she sat back down at the table.

"And you're not going to be able to drive anymore, right?" Pete held a slice of buttered bread in one hand and his soup spoon in the other.

"No. I'll drive, but now I need to stop around 3:30. It's a little much to expect Emily to cook a company dinner."

Pete took another bite of bread. "Well, after today you won't have to drive. I've taken care of it, I think."

"What do you mean, you've taken care of it?" Bob pushed his chair away from the table.

"Dana called—"

Charlotte nodded.

"—I left her a message this morning to see if she knew of anyone who needed a job. I figured since she knew all the high school kids, she might know someone who wants a job. She has a student who's interested; he just has to talk it over with his mom."

"Well, that's nice, Pete." Charlotte smiled. It sounded like a good plan. "Who's the student?" Charlotte asked.

"His mom grew up here. Dana said he's from a good family."

"What's the boy's name?"

"His last name is Matthews."

"*Sean* Matthews?" Charlotte's spoon clattered to the table.

"I don't know, exactly." Pete rubbed his chin. "I'm not sure if Dana said what his first name was."

"Oh, Pete."

"You think it's that kid, the *Sean* that Emily has a crush on? The one Sam told me about?" Pete rubbed his chin again.

Charlotte nodded.

"What kid?" Bob asked. "What are you talking about?"

Charlotte just shook her head.

CHARLOTTE SLIPPED INTO THE HOUSE at 3:15 after her last trip to the elevator. She poked her head into the family room and found Bob sound asleep in his chair. A moment later she was back in the kitchen assessing what she could pull together for dinner. The blinking light on the answering machine caught her attention. She pushed the button just as a car pulled up to the back door.

The first message was from Rosemary asking how Bob was doing.

Bill came through the door and left it open. Jennifer and Madison yelled for Toby and then laughed and squealed. "We're early," Bill said.

"Hi." Charlotte gave him a quick hug. "I'm just listening to my messages."

She'd missed the first part of the second message. It sounded like Dana. "—call this afternoon. He's very grateful for the possibility of a job."

"What's that about?" Bill asked.

Charlotte shook her head. "Shhh."

The third message had started. "—Sean Matthews. I'm Rayann's brother. She and Emily are friends." His voice sounded nervous. "I heard that you're looking for someone to drive truck during harvest, part-time. I'm interested. Please call me back." He left his phone number and then paused. "Oh, this message is for Pete. Pete Stevenson."

Charlotte saved the message.

"So Pete's in charge now?" Bill rolled up the sleeves of his dress shirt. "What about Sam? Why can't he drive? He should be earning his keep around here." Bill opened the cookie jar and pulled out a snickerdoodle.

Earning his keep? "Shhh," Charlotte said again. "I have one more message."

This time it was a man's voice. "Hello, Mr. and Mrs. Stevenson. This is Coach Williams. I want Sam to play, but I just found out his grades aren't quite up to school standards. Give me a call. I want to run something by you."

"So," Bill rubbed his hands together, "Sam *could* be playing football if his grades were better? Good grief."

Charlotte really wished Bill hadn't heard the messages.

"How come you're here so early?"

"Several of the people I was supposed to meet with didn't show." He shrugged. "We had to reschedule. It doesn't do me any good to only talk with some of them."

"That's too bad."

"Not really. They get a bill either way." Bill smiled. "Where's Dad?"

"Asleep in his chair." Charlotte picked up the phone.

"Come here, girl!" It was Madison yelling for Toby again. "I have the stick!"

Bill headed into the family room.

Charlotte called the high school, hoping she could catch Coach Williams before he left for practice. The secretary transferred her to the gym.

"Here's the deal," Coach Williams said. "Sam's grades are borderline. I checked with all of his teachers and they want to give him a chance, so we're putting him on academic probation."

"What does that mean?" Charlotte asked.

"His grades get better within the next two weeks, or he doesn't play."

"Have you talked with him about it?" Charlotte asked.

"That's what I'm going to do next. But I wanted to suggest that you get the kid a tutor, a.s.a.p."

"Okay." Charlotte shifted the phone to her other ear. "But has Sam agreed to play football?"

Bill walked back into the kitchen.

"He's been practicing with the team all week," Williams' voice boomed.

Bill looked puzzled. He mouthed, "What's going on?"

Charlotte turned her head. "I'll look into a tutor, Coach, and we're looking forward to watching him play. Thank you."

"Oh, and did Sam tell you practice is ending early tonight? We're done at 4:30."

"No." Of course Sam hadn't told her. It was one of many details that he seemed to overlook.

"The assistant coach and I are going to go spy on Sheridan."

"Is everything all right?" Bill asked as Charlotte hung up the phone.

"I think so. Except practice is ending early."

"I'll still pick him up," Bill said. "I'm looking forward to hearing all about him playing football."

Charlotte nodded.

"Besides, it will give me a chance to get to know my nephew better." Bill took another cookie from the jar. "What else did the coach say? About Sam's grades?"

"He just needs a little help with his classes."

Bill rubbed his hands together. "I'm going to go wake Dad up and give him the good news."

"Let him sleep. We don't even know for sure that Sam's going to play." *What if Sam decided not to play?*

"What do you mean? You heard it from the coach!" Bill laughed.

"It's not that simple." Charlotte turned toward the backdoor. "I need to go see my girls." She stepped out into the yard. Toby was chasing both girls across the yard.

"Grandma!" The girls rushed toward her.

Charlotte hugged her granddaughters. "Show me how much you've grown."

They both stood on tiptoes, back to back.

"Oh my!" Charlotte put a hand on each of their heads. "You're going to be up to my chin in no time." Madison was younger, but she was nearly as tall as Jennifer.

The girls giggled. "Where's Emily?" Madison asked.

"Coming home on the bus. She should be here any minute. Let's hurry down to the stop."

The girls skipped ahead with Toby barking at their heels, and Charlotte walked beside Bill. "How is Anna?"

"Good. She's busy with the girls and redecorating the family room, with her mom's help."

"And how's the town of River Bend?"

"We have a new bond measure on the November ballot that's keeping me busy. We need it to pass to put in new restrooms at the park." Bill picked up a stick, threw it for Toby, and then held out his dusty hands. He looked down at his suit.

Charlotte offered him her sleeve. "It won't matter. I've been driving truck all day. Wipe your hands on my shirt."

Bill complied. "Work's going well. The property I looked at today is part of an estate sale. It's a big operation, four thousand acres."

"But no heirs?"

"Plenty of heirs." Toby brought the stick back to Bill. "But none who want to farm."

Charlotte took the stick from the dog and hurled it into the air. "What a shame."

They reached the road just as the mail carrier pulled away from their mailbox, honking his horn. Charlotte waved as she retrieved the mail. He honked every day to let her know she could walk out to the box, although these days Christopher usually beat her to it. A minute later the bus arrived. Christopher climbed down, alone again.

"Where's Emily?" Charlotte asked quietly. Bill had already overheard enough for one day.

"At the back of the bus. Watching you-know-who."

Charlotte leaned back. There, following the bus, was Sean's Mustang. Rayann was with him.

Charlotte pointed Christopher toward his cousins. "Look who's here."

Christopher gave them a small wave, hugged Toby, found a stick, and threw it in the direction of the house. All three children ran after the dog. "Not too fast," Bill called after Jennifer and Madison.

Finally, Emily sauntered off the bus.

Sean turned his Mustang in behind them, driving slowly. He rolled down his window and stopped the car. "Hello, Mrs. Stevenson."

"Hello." She introduced Bill to him.

Emily stepped toward the car.

Sean stuck his hand through the window and shook Bill's hand. "I wanted to talk with you about that truck-driving job. Did you get my message?"

"That's the wrong uncle." Emily wrinkled her nose. "It's Uncle Pete that knows Miss Simons."

"Miss Simons?" Bill turned toward his mother.

"Dana Simons," Charlotte answered. "She left the message earlier."

Bill hooted. "That little chubby thing Pete used to date?"

"Bill." Charlotte crossed her arms. "She's not chubby, and she never was chubby. In fact, she's quite attractive."

"Oh." Bill smirked.

"Sean." Charlotte stepped forward. "Pete is out in the field."

"I can take them down." Emily shifted her book bag to her other shoulder.

Charlotte cleared her throat.

"I'd really like the job, Mrs. Stevenson."

"Go ahead and park by the house." Charlotte wasn't sure whether she was doing the right thing. "Then go with Emily to talk to Pete." Had she just put Sean's best interest before her granddaughter's?

Chapter Sixteen

Emily felt giddy leading Sean and Rayann down the road toward the barn. "That's Stormy." She pointed to the middle of the pasture. "Isn't she beautiful?" The foal lifted her head and swung her tail. A slight breeze ruffled her mane.

"I've always wanted a horse." Rayann sighed.

"You've always wanted everything," Sean said. "A horse. A trip to Hawaii. A Nordstrom charge card."

"Stop." Rayann kicked a rock toward her brother.

"Pete's down in the home quarter. They got a little behind since Grandpa had his accident." Emily's voice dropped. "I guess Pete's been driving the combine and filling up the truck and then driving it to the elevator."

"A one-man band," Sean said.

"Something like that." Emily pushed up the sleeves of the Cornhuskers sweatshirt. It was hot, but she didn't want to pull it over her head and mess up her hair.

"How many acres do your grandparents have?" Sean asked.

Was it a thousand? Suddenly Emily couldn't remember. "A lot." She giggled.

They turned into the field and walked over the stubble. Dust began to cover Emily's Pumas. She should have changed into her boots. A grasshopper flew up from the ground, and Emily batted it away.

When they got close to the combine, Pete jumped down and shook Sean's hand. "What's your experience?" he asked without any preamble. Sean surveyed the fields around him.

"I drove a truck during wheat harvest for my uncle."

"Well, when can you start? I needed someone yesterday."

"Right now." Sean smiled.

"You're hired." Pete extended his hand again.

Emily couldn't help but smile along with him. She couldn't believe Sean was going to be working around the farm for a while. How lucky could you get? She beamed as she and Rayann walked back to the house, picking their way through the stubble and swatting grasshoppers away from their faces.

"I better go call Mom," Rayann said, "to tell her we'll be late."

"How about if we go pet the horses after you're done?" Emily said.

Later, as Emily and Rayann led Jennifer and Madison by their dust-covered hands away from the horses back to the house and toward the smell of dinner, Bill's car pulled into the driveway. He and Sam stepped out.

"How was football? Has Coach Williams told you not to bother yet?" Emily said to Sam.

Emily rolled her eyes, but Rayann perked up.

"Football? Cool," Rayann said. "Maybe I'll go to the game."

"We can't go this Friday, but we'll be there for homecoming." Uncle Bill patted Sam on the back. "He might be a chip off the old block after all. Football. It's the best sport in the world."

Emily expected Sam to disagree, but he didn't say anything. "Sam," she said, "what did you used to tell me all the time about soccer?"

He shrugged.

"How many people in the world play?" Emily felt driven to prove Bill wrong.

"Two hundred forty million people from two hundred countries. That's almost as many people as in the entire US." Sam's voice was monotone. "A whole lot more people play soccer than American football."

"That's nice, Sam." Bill spread his arms wide. "But do you see anyone playing soccer around here?" He laughed.

Sam just grunted and pushed open the back door, and Bill followed. As soon as the door shut behind them, Rayann turned to Emily. "That was really awkward with your uncle," Rayann whispered. "I like the other one better."

"Pete?"

Rayann used a normal tone. "Even if he didn't graduate. Just kidding. Seriously, you should talk to him about getting his GED. I bet they have a program at Harding, maybe even at the college. It would really impress Miss Simons."

Emily shook her head. Uncle Pete would never want to do that.

Chapter Seventeen

"Who wants a piece of apple crisp?" Charlotte asked. Everyone at the table, except for Emily, did. Sam asked if he could be excused to take a quick shower and eat his dessert as soon as he was done.

"Please!" Bill boomed. "I was wondering when you were going to get cleaned up."

Charlotte started a pot of coffee and returned with the crisp and a stack of dessert plates.

"So," Bill said, turning to Christopher. "How's school going?"

"Fine. I'm working on a report on natural disasters."

"Impressive," Bill said. "Like hurricanes and typhoons?"

"More like earthquakes."

"How about tornadoes?" Bill asked. "That's a real local topic."

"I might include tornadoes." Christopher paused. "Maybe."

Charlotte cut the dessert. She'd been avoiding the topic of tornadoes with Christopher, not wanting to start a new obsession. The boy had a way of fixating on things.

"If you decide to, you'll have some primary sources right here, around this table, starting with Pete." Bill slapped the table.

"Really?" Christopher's eyes grew wide.

"Pete, remember when you used to chase tornadoes?"

Charlotte shook her head. "Bill, that's enough."

"Uncle Pete chased storms?" Christopher stood, his mouth dropping open.

"No. Not really." Pete ducked his head.

"Pete." Bill drew out his brother's name.

"Can I go with you next time there's one around here?" Christopher rocked from foot to foot.

"No. No chasing tornadoes." Pete ate a bite of his crisp. "Mom, this is delicious."

Jennifer and Madison slipped out of their chairs and began chasing Lightning around the table. The cat let out a loud meow when they finally caught him.

"Don't let that thing scratch you." Bill pushed back his chair.

"Grandma, where are the dolls?" Jennifer asked, vigorously petting the cat.

"In the basket on the landing."

Christopher watched them walk away with his kitten and then got up to follow them. "What are you going to do to Lightning?" he asked.

Jennifer giggled but kept walking.

"Emily, would you keep an eye on them?" Charlotte asked, heading toward the counter for the second pot of coffee. Emily sighed and followed the little girls up the stairs.

"So, what brings you to the farm today?" Pete asked Bill.

Bill started talking about the farm in Monroe County. "No one in the family wants it because the farm hasn't been profitable in years, even though it's so big."

"Things are turning around." Bob put his elbows on the table. "The price of ethanol is making farming profitable again, at least corn."

"But if farming isn't in their blood, it doesn't matter if there's a living in it or not." Pete stood. "You have to have a passion for it. Right, Bill?"

Bill smirked. "I have a passion for the property."

Charlotte sat back down at the table and poured herself a mug of coffee.

"But not the work." Pete didn't give Bill a chance to answer. "Because it is a lot of work. It's a big investment to keep a farm going. Not a lot of security in it either, especially when big brother comes snooping around, eyeing the place."

"Pete," Charlotte murmured. "Please."

"Good grief," Bill said. "I'm not eyeing this place. I'm just being practical. We can't keep our heads in the clouds forever."

"I don't want to talk about that now." Bob stirred his coffee and turned his head toward Pete. "I want to talk about that new driver you hired."

"Sean?" Pete rubbed his chin.

"Seems like you hired him in a rush, son," Bob said.

Pete nodded. "Well, we are in a rush. It's harvest time. We're down a driver."

"I hope you won't regret it."

"Emily seems smitten by the young man." Bill put a

second cube of sugar in his coffee. "He seems like a nice enough kid, though."

"He's three years older than Emily." Charlotte wondered if Bill had any idea of how things worked. He hadn't dated much, except for homecoming and prom, until college.

Sam stopped in the doorway, his hair wet and wavy from the shower.

"The thing with Sean is that he gets out of school at lunch because he only needs three classes to graduate," Pete said. "And he has experience."

Sam shook his head. "Emily's going to love having him around all the time."

"Emily will be fine." Pete rubbed his chin. "I'll talk with her."

"Emily doesn't listen to anyone." Sam headed into the kitchen.

Charlotte stared into her coffee. Maybe Emily's crush on Sean wouldn't last long. He didn't seem to encourage it. At least that was a good thing.

Bill turned toward Bob. "I'll let the farm talk go for now, but there's something you and Mom need to do, and soon, especially considering your recent hospital stay."

"What's that?" Bob asked.

"Make your wills."

"We have wills."

"From years ago. You need new ones. You didn't have dependent minors when you made them before, right?"

Bob grunted and added more milk to his coffee.

"You need to plan for their futures, and you need to designate a guardian."

"Guardian?" Pete said.

"Yes, guardian. To take responsibility for the kids in case something happens to Mom and Dad."

"I know what a guardian is." Pete glared at Bill. "That's what I would be if anything happened to Mom and Dad."

"You!" Bill thumped the table. "You don't know anything about kids."

Pete pushed his chair back and pulled his cap over his forehead. "I have work to do, more farmwork, to support this family. I'm out of here."

"What's with him?" Bill asked.

The back door slammed.

"Bill." Charlotte stood. "That's enough."

"Hey, I'm just looking out for everyone's best interest. Especially the kids."

"We'll talk about all of this later." Charlotte glanced at Bob. He was licking his fork, probably relishing every bit of his tiny piece of crisp. Was he oblivious to what Bill was saying?

"Later doesn't cut it with wills, Mom. I can't tell you—"

"Bill, Dad and I will talk about this at another time."

Charlotte turned toward the kitchen for the pot of coffee. Sam stood on the other side of the fridge drinking a glass of milk. "What was Uncle Bill talking about?" Sam asked.

"Nothing. He's just talking."

"Does he want to be our guardian?"

Charlotte shook her head, but she really didn't know what Bill wanted.

Chapter Eighteen

Emily sat at the computer with a document open. In the right hand corner she typed: Emily Slater/Freshman English/Persuasive Essay. In the middle of the paper she wrote: Why You Should Be a Vegetarian.

She set her fingers on the keyboard, but the words wouldn't come. She thought for a moment and then clicked open the Web browser.

Then she Googled "GED programs Harding Nebraska." Rayann was right. Harding College did offer a GED. She printed out the information and then clicked back to her homework. She needed to turn in an outline tomorrow.

She heard Grandma and Sam talking in the dining room. Emily stopped typing and started listening.

"My grades are fine," Sam said.

"They're not," Grandma insisted. "You're on academic probation."

"So what's the worst thing that can happen? I'll get kicked off the team, that's all."

"Sam, did you tell your coach that you wanted to play?"

"I never told him I didn't."

"Well then," Grandma said. "If you don't want to play,

don't, but if you do make a commitment, you need to follow through with it."

Emily leaned closer, trying to hear more. Grandma's voice softened. "Do you want to drive?"

Emily couldn't hear Sam's answer.

"You can call Pastor Nathan and see if he can still tutor you."

"I don't want to call him."

There was a long pause and then Sam said, his voice a little louder, "Grandma, would you call him?"

Now Emily couldn't hear Grandma's answer. She turned her attention back to her outline. A couple of minutes later, Grandma came into the room and told her it was time for bed.

"I just have to finish this outline and then print it out." Emily swiveled around. "Grandma, may Rayann come over after school tomorrow and stay for dinner? Then she can ride to the football game with us, or with Sean if he gets done in time."

"I don't know what we're going to have for dinner."

"It doesn't matter," Emily said. Was Grandma stalling? "Rayann's not picky. She's not a vegetarian or anything like that." Emily smiled.

Grandma nodded. "I guess that's okay." Emily braced herself to answer questions about Ashley, but Grandma turned and walked out of the room.

Ashley had been acting even weirder at school, and Emily hadn't sat by her at lunch for a couple of days now. Sam rushed into the family room. "Get off the computer." He pulled the back of the chair. "It's my turn."

"Did you leave your homework until the last minute?" Emily asked.

"I don't have any homework."

"Right." She slid closer to the desk, pulling the chair from Sam's hand.

"I have research I need to do," he said.

"On what?"

"On *who* is more like it."

"On whom." Emily took her essay and the GED info out of the printer. "Whom are you researching?"

"It's none of your business."

Emily headed to the hall. He was probably trying to find one of his old friends on Facebook.

"Hey, Em." All of a sudden Sam sounded halfway nice for a change, so she stopped. "If something happened to Grandma and Grandpa, where would you want to live?"

"What a stupid thing to ask."

"No, it's not. Where would you want to live?"

"California, probably. Maybe here, on the farm."

"What if we couldn't stay here?"

"California then."

Emily headed upstairs. What was Sam up to? And why was he so moody?

Chapter Nineteen

Charlotte parked the car across the street from the football field, and Christopher and Bob climbed out in a hurry. "I don't want to miss the kickoff," Bob said, hobbling across the pavement. Christopher followed.

Charlotte turned off the motor and Emily and Rayann climbed slowly from the backseat. Emily turned around and looked down the road. Was she looking for Sean? He had been taking one last load to the elevator when they left for the game but had said he was going to come.

"There's Ashley," Charlotte said, pointing across the street. Ashley waved. "Brace yourself," Rayann whispered.

Charlotte turned. Were they talking about Ashley?

There was a pause as the girls exchanged a look.

"We're going to wait out here for a couple of minutes and stretch our legs," Emily said. "The backseat was a little cramped with Christopher sitting between us."

Rayann pulled down the sleeves of her blouse and shivered. "Besides, Sean has my jacket in his car. I'm going to need it."

Charlotte scanned the bleachers. Bob sat a space over from Rosemary, obviously leaving room for Charlotte. Christopher sat in front of Bob. Rosemary stood and began waving. Charlotte waved back and made her way up the stairs. Pastor Nathan sat on the other side of Rosemary. He was waving too.

The teams were still warming up. Charlotte hadn't missed a thing.

"Bob says the doctor cleared him." Rosemary patted Charlotte's arm as she lowered herself onto the bleacher.

Charlotte nodded. "Isn't that great news?"

"Charlotte." Pastor Nathan leaned forward. "I got your message. I'd be happy to."

"Thank you."

Rosemary shot Charlotte a puzzled look. "What's that about?"

"I'll tell you later." She let her eyes drift to the field, where the players were warming up.

Rosemary crossed her arms and then looked around. "Where's Pete?"

"He should be here—"

"Shhh." Bob pointed to the field. Sam was poised to kick the ball, looking so grown-up in his football jersey, his shoulders wide and powerful. He took a run and—pow!— sent the ball sailing straight through the goalposts. "He's good." Bob beamed.

Charlotte felt a stab of grief for Denise. Oh, the things she was missing.

Poor Brendan hobbled around on the sidelines. Sam readied himself for another kick.

"Watch," Bob said, shushing Rosemary as she began to speak.

All three of them sat in silence. Charlotte couldn't remember the last time Bob was so excited about something. She smiled. She would enjoy it as long as it lasted.

The ball hit the right post and fell to the ground. "Oh, well." Bob leaned back. "You can't win 'em all."

After the *Star-Spangled Banner* the Sheridan High School football team kicked off. Charlotte watched Sam standing by Brendan on the sidelines. The other boys drifted away from him.

Just as Bedford got a first down, Pete arrived and sat in front of Charlotte. Emily and Rayann, followed by Sean, headed to the student section a few minutes later. Ashley waved at them and scooted over, but the three sat down a few rows in front of Ashley. Charlotte frowned. "You're going to get a kink in your neck," Rosemary teased.

A few minutes later, Dana Simons arrived and sat beside Mr. Santos down in the first row. She turned around and waved. Charlotte waved back, and Pete crossed his arms. Bedford stopped the other team at the fifteen-yard line. It was back and forth, but no touchdowns, and no kicking or punting for Sam.

Sam kicked off the second half, a decent kick, but the Sheridan offense caught it and ran. Sam stepped backward after the kickoff, and then followed his teammates as they ran forward, but he looked unsure of himself, holding his arms at his side. The Sheridan fullback headed up the sidelines, and Sam reached out to tackle the runner, grabbing his shirt, but the guy slipped away.

At the end of the third quarter, Bedford scored and missed the point after. In the middle of the fourth quarter,

Sam took a chance on a field goal. The Sheridan linebackers rushed and blocked the kick. He walked off the field, his helmet in his hands.

Poor Sam. Charlotte glanced at Bob. He looked worse than his grandson as they stood to go.

Pete started down the bleachers ahead of the rest of them. Mr. Santos was gone, and Dana was sitting alone. Pete stopped and said something to her. Dana smiled.

Chapter Twenty

Emily heard a noise and raised her head an inch off her pillow, and then dropped it back down. Sunlight spread through her sheer curtains, giving a rosy glow to the room. Had Grandma let her sleep in?

"Rise and shine!" Christopher yelled as he flung open her bedroom door.

"Knock first!" Emily pulled the covers over her head.

"The calves got out again." Christopher yanked the blankets away from her face.

"The calves are always out."

"I helped this time. Sam was still asleep. Sean and me fixed it."

"Sean and I." Emily sat up. "Sean's here?"

"Driving the truck."

"I didn't think they were harvesting today."

"Every day but Sunday, is what Pete says."

Sean. That was why Grandma didn't wake her.

"Get out of my room." As Emily climbed out of bed, her quilt tangled around her feet. She took a step and stumbled. "What's Sam doing?"

"He just got up too. He's a little grumpy though."

Emily flung her blankets onto the bed and hiked up her pink-and-red-striped pajama bottoms. *Football.* Everyone was grumpy last night, at least all the men. What was Sam thinking playing football anyway? She pulled underwear from the pile of clothes on her chair. Christopher covered his eyes and ran from the room.

Emily slammed the door after him.

After her shower, she headed down to get started on her chores. The horses were probably really hungry.

Grandma sat at the table, a cookbook spread open in front of her.

"Hi." Emily leaned against the counter. "What are you doing?"

"Figuring out what to fix for dinner tonight." Grandma looked up at Emily. "What are your plans for the day?"

"Well, I'm going to start with my chores." She poured a glass of milk from the pitcher in the fridge. "I was wondering if Rayann could come out."

Grandma shook her head. "Not today. I need your help because Bill and Anna and the girls are coming for dinner, remember?"

Emily slumped onto a chair.

"We have chores. The calves got out again this morning. Grandpa has more fence to repair." Grandma closed the cookbook. "We have too much going on."

EMILY FED THE HORSES and looked in the hay in the barn for the little cats. Two ran out, a gray one that looked like Lightning and a pure black one. They were nearly grown, but still leggy and jumpy as they scurried to and fro.

She opened the door to the tack room and took a deep breath as she entered. She loved the smell of the room: the leather and wool and hay and hint of horse sweat from years gone by, and the old, seasoned boards of the barn. Even the silver on the bridles seemed to give off a metallic scent, mixed in with the musty smell that permeated everything.

Emily swung her leg over the saddle on the saddle tree. She felt connected to her mother in the tack room, even more so than in her bedroom, the room her mother had slept in all those years ago. Maybe it was because the tack room hadn't changed; it had all the things her mother had touched and used.

The gray cat slipped through the cracked door and threw himself at Emily's leg. She squealed and grabbed it, taking it with her back into the barn.

Next she headed to the chicken coop and gathered the eggs in the plastic pail, tiptoeing around the coop, pinching her nose with her finger and thumb. It needed to be cleaned out. She was surprised Grandma didn't add it to her list of Saturday chores.

She headed back to the house for a glass of water. The phone was ringing when she entered. "I'll get it!" Emily yelled, not sure if anyone else was even in the house, but she was sure that it would be Rayann.

Emily slumped into a dining room chair. It was Ashley. "Hey, Emily." Ashley's voice was as bubbly as always. "I wanted to apologize."

Emily sat up straight.

"I've felt bad about that day in the cafeteria. My feelings were hurt, because, well, because you've been hanging out with Rayann, and then when I tried to talk more about your grandpa you cut me off."

Emily's heart began to pound. This was why grown-ups liked Ashley so much; she always did the right thing.

"Don't worry about it," Emily said.

There was a pause. Did Ashley expect her to apologize too? For hanging out with Rayann? For feeling scared about Grandpa?

"So, do you want to come over?" Ashley asked. "Or I could go over to your place."

Emily thought for a minute. Grandma said no to Rayann, but Grandma liked Ashley better, that was for sure. Grandma would probably let Ashley come over and justify it because Ashley would help with the chores or fix dinner or something. On the other hand, Emily wasn't sure if she wanted Ashley to come over. It all felt too awkward. She knew she didn't want to go to Ashley's, not with Sean at Heather Creek Farm.

"I can't. Grandma wouldn't let Rayann come over, so I don't think she's going to say yes now."

"Okay." Ashley's voice was quiet. "I'll see you at church then."

Emily felt unsettled as she hung up the phone. A splash of water crested the rim of the glass and sloshed onto her shirt.

"Emily!" It was Grandma, yelling from the chicken yard. "I have another chore for you."

Emily shuffled through the house and put the glass in the sink. A couple minutes later she faced Grandma.

"I need you and Christopher to clean out the chicken coop; I didn't realize how filthy it was getting until I poked my head in there. Next time let me know," Grandma said.

Emily made a face. *Yuck.* And then she decided to forge ahead with what she'd been wondering. "Ashley called to see if she could come over, but I told her no, because you wouldn't let Rayann come over today."

"That's right," Grandma answered, shading her eyes against the sun.

"But you would rather have Ashley over instead of Rayann, right?" Emily knew she was on the verge of picking a fight. It's something she would have said to her mom. "I mean if I'd asked about Ashley first, you would have let her come over. Right?"

Grandma shoved her hands in the pockets of her jacket. "I do think, perhaps, that Ashley is a better influence than Rayann. But, as I already told you, we have too much to do today to have company."

Emily rolled her eyes. Yeah, right. She didn't believe Grandma for one second. She wheeled around toward the house.

"I'll be at the house in just a minute. I need you to help me get lunch on the table," Grandma called out after her, ignoring her antics. Emily hated having her outbursts ignored even more than being scolded. She scooped up her hair and twisted it on top of her hair, securing it with a hair band that she pulled from her wrist as she stomped across the lawn.

She had the table set by the time Grandma came into the house. "Put the pot of soup on the stove, please." Grandma took off her jacket. "We'll have sandwiches too."

A half hour later, Sean pulled his truck into the driveway. Emily stood at the kitchen window, ready to open the back door.

"Put the milk on the table," Grandma instructed Emily.

Pete came in through the back door, laughing, followed by Christopher and then Sean. Sean wore a long-sleeve blue T-shirt that made his eyes even brighter than usual. He smiled at her, and Emily felt all shaky inside. "So how's the truck driving going?" Charlotte asked.

"Fine," Sean said. He seemed intimidated, something that Emily hadn't seen in him before.

"I bet it beats a boring old Saturday afternoon in Lincoln by a long shot, huh?" Pete slapped his back.

Emily set the milk on the table roughly, and a little splashed onto Grandma's quilted runner. Emily grabbed the napkin at her place and dabbed at the fabric. She wished that she was in Lincoln this afternoon, with Rayann and Sean. She wished that she could be anywhere but in the chicken coop on Heather Creek Farm, her destination for this particular afternoon.

Chapter Twenty-One

Charlotte twisted the last crescent roll and then covered the metal tray with plastic. The rolls would be ready to bake in a couple of hours, just in time for dinner.

A car turned into the driveway. She glanced at the clock. Four PM. Bill and Anna and the girls were right on time.

She took off her apron, draped it over a chair, and opened the back door.

Anna stood next to the side of the car as Jennifer and Madison climbed out.

"Where's Emily?" Jennifer called out.

"She and Christopher are cleaning the chicken coop."

"Ooh, fun!" Jennifer started running.

Madison looked up at her mother.

"Jennifer, wait," Anna yelled. "You didn't bring a change of clothes."

Jennifer shuffled back to her mother.

Bill stepped around the car and hugged Charlotte. He wore jeans and a polo shirt. Charlotte realized that it had been months since she'd seen him wearing anything except a suit and tie. "I thought I'd hang out with Pete and Dad for a little while."

"They're up in the north quarter," Charlotte said, shading her eyes from the afternoon sun.

"Emily and Christopher should be about done," Charlotte told the girls.

"I guess we could walk down to the chickens, just as long as we don't go inside the gate," Anna said.

"Let's go," Charlotte said. "We'll just check to see if they're almost done." She turned toward Anna. "And then I need to go into town and pick up a few things for dinner. Want to go with me?"

"I could ride along." Anna pulled gloves from her pocket and slipped them on her hands. "If you think Emily can be trusted to watch the girls."

"She can," Charlotte spoke quietly so the little girls couldn't hear.

As they neared the coop, Emily's voice screeched. "What a bunch of—"

"Emily," Charlotte called out, drowning out her granddaughter's voice as she opened the gate.

Anna frowned.

Christopher poked his head out of the coop. "Oh, hi." He flung a shovel of manure into the wheelbarrow.

Emily stepped out of the coop. "Do we dump this on the garden?" Fine white feathers stuck to her hair.

"In the pile by the garden."

"So what's the point?"

"Grandpa will turn it into the soil after we clean up the garden in a few weeks."

"Oh." Emily ducked back into the coop.

"Emily." Charlotte followed her in. "You need to say hello to Anna and the girls."

Emily poked her head back out. "Hi, all."

"Emily, I was wondering if you would watch the girls while Charlotte and I run into town?" Anna smiled sweetly.

"Now?" Emily scraped her shovel along the cement floor. Two hens flew up to the beam.

"No, in a few minutes," Charlotte answered. In fact, it looked like they were almost done; all they needed to do was empty the wheelbarrow.

"I guess I don't have anything better to do, do I?"

A hen flapped toward the fence frantically. Madison squealed. The hen squawked and took flight and then tried to land on the fence.

"I want to go back to the house," Madison said, hiding behind her mother's leg.

"It's just a chicken." Jennifer began flapping her arms.

"Jennifer." Anna's voice was firm. "Stop that now."

AFTER FINISHING UP at the grocery store, Anna asked Charlotte if they could stop for a cup of coffee.

Charlotte checked her watch. It was 4:45. "I should have dinner on the table by six thirty. I guess we could, if we're quick."

"I didn't sleep very well. I just need a little caffeine." Anna brushed an imaginary piece of lint from her tailored jacket as they stepped into Mel's Place. "Just a little pick-me-up."

Anna wiggled out of her jacket and draped it over her chair as Melody greeted the two women. Anna sat down and twisted her ring on her finger for a moment, fingering the diamond.

"Is everything okay?" Charlotte knew her daughter-in-law well enough to tell when she was nervous.

"What was that all about? Emily saying she didn't have anything better to do than watch the girls?"

"She wanted to have a friend over."

"Is she grounded?"

"No."

"Bill said she's interested in the boy driving the truck for Pete." Anna brushed her dark hair away from her face. "And she's, what, an eighth grader?"

"A freshman."

"Oh. Still." Anna's tone of voice made Charlotte tense. "Are you worried that she'll end up like Denise?"

Charlotte took a deep breath.

"You know," Anna whispered.

Of course that was what she was worried about, but Charlotte wasn't going to admit it to Anna. "I don't want her to get romantically—emotionally—involved at this age, at all."

Melody took their order and then brought two coffees to the table.

Anna leaned forward. "Bill has said, over and over, how boy-crazy Denise was and how you all saw it coming."

Charlotte leaned back. The last thing she wanted to do was gossip, seventeen years later, about her dead daughter.

"So," Charlotte said, brightening, "how's school going for the girls?"

"Oh, great," Anna gushed. "You know, those granddaughters of yours are just the smartest things." She picked up her spoon and tapped it on the table.

Melody arrived with a plate. "A chocolate-caramel tart," she announced. "My special recipe and my special treat."

"Thank you!" Charlotte reached for one.

Anna shook her head. "Ooh, they look good, but I'm going to have to pass. I'm on a sugar fast."

"Oh dear." Melody looked concerned. "You poor thing."

"No, I'm fine. And I have so much more energy."

"Really?" Melody tilted her head. "Now that's hard to imagine. Life without chocolate. Well, let me know if I can get you anything else."

"Could I have some skim milk for my coffee?" Anna held her spoon in midair and turned back to Charlotte. "Now, Bill said that he spoke to you about redoing your will and appointing guardians for the kids."

Charlotte took a bite of the tart.

"Anyway, we don't want you two to have to worry about that, not at all."

Charlotte swallowed. The tart was divine. "We haven't worried about it. We haven't even thought about it, not even after Bill mentioned it the other day."

Melody delivered a little china pitcher of milk.

"This is delicious!" Charlotte held up her half-eaten treat.

Melody mouthed, "Thank you."

"As far as being guardians—"

"Anna, I don't think we should discuss this before I've talked with Bob." Charlotte took another bite of the tart.

Anna pursed her lips and poured the watery milk into her coffee, busying herself with stirring the mixture around and around.

Charlotte tried to savor the chocolate and caramel. The other night Bill seemed to think he and Anna should be the children's guardians, but Charlotte couldn't fathom the children wanting to live with Bill and Anna.

But who *would* she and Bob choose? And why were Bill and Anna so interested in this now?

Chapter Twenty-Two

After dinner Charlotte sat down in her chair to listen to Madison. Sam was already at the computer, checking his Facebook page.

"I brought *The Boxcar Children*," Madison said, pulling it from the backpack that she had brought along. "Do you want to listen to me read, Christopher?" she asked.

He shook his head. "I don't like those books." He left the room. A moment later the front door opened and then closed.

Anna raised her eyebrows. "What was that all about?"

"Could be the subject matter," Sam answered without turning his head. "A group of siblings lose their parents."

"Still." Anna sat down on the couch next to Bill. "Go ahead, Madison."

Madison began to read. Jennifer pulled out a game from the shelf and tugged on Emily's shirt. Emily nodded and they headed toward the dining room. After a few minutes of flawless reading Madison stopped and turned toward her mom. "I want to play with Emily. May I stop reading?"

Anna nodded.

"That was great, sweetie." Charlotte gave her granddaughter a hug. Bob turned the volume up on the TV. It was the fourth quarter of the Cornhuskers game. Pete came in from milking and sat on the floor.

"Mom, Dad, have you thought about what I said about redoing your will?" Bill asked as a car commercial came on.

"We haven't had a chance to talk." Charlotte said quickly. Bob didn't turn his head. He was engrossed in the commercial.

"Not this again." Pete struggled to his feet, bumping against the table lamp.

Bill put out his hand to steady it. "I'm just thinking about the practical matters involved with Mom and Dad parenting again."

"I'm going to go check on Christopher," Charlotte said, picking up Madison's book and placing it by her purse.

"You wouldn't have to worry about relocating the kids." Bill said. "We'd move here."

Sam spun around on the desk chair. Bob slowly turned his head. "What?"

"Well, I won't be mayor forever, and..."

"But I'm already here." Pete leaned against the doorway to the hall.

"Bill," Anna practically hissed, "we didn't *talk* about moving *here*."

"And Bob and I haven't talked about anything, so the subject is closed." Charlotte headed out of the room.

"Bill, are you planning on something happening to Mom and Dad?" Pete moved to let Charlotte into the hallway.

"Don't be ridiculous. I'm just looking out after everyone's best interest. Someone has to."

"Christopher," Charlotte yelled from the porch. "Come in; it's too dark out here."

Toby barked. A moment later Christopher appeared, walking away from the fence. "I was watching the calves," he said. "Making sure none of them escaped."

"Emily is playing a board game with the girls. Do you want to play?"

He shrugged.

"I thought I'd see if they would let me play too."

"Okay," he answered.

The girls had just started a game of Life, but they were happy to start over to include Charlotte and Christopher.

The football game ended and the men began to stir. Bill's voice boomed, "What are you doing? Googling yourself?" Was he talking to Sam?

Charlotte couldn't hear Sam's response.

"I do that sometimes," Bill said. "Just to see what's out there." He laughed.

"I *wasn't* Googling myself." Sam's voice was quiet. Charlotte couldn't make out the rest of what he said.

A moment later, Bill stood at the table with his hand on Anna's shoulder. "Chris, how's the tornado research going?"

Christopher sighed. "Pete keeps avoiding my questions."

Bill laughed again. "Well, if he doesn't talk to you in a few days give me a call. I'll give you all the details."

Chapter Twenty-Three

Emily latched the gate to the chicken yard.

"Hey, Em, can we talk?" Uncle Pete was up early, for a Sunday. He strode across the road, his boots kicking up the dust.

"What's up?" she asked, swinging the pail of eggs to her right hand.

"I've been meaning to talk to you for a few days."

Emily blushed.

"It doesn't seem like it has been, you know, a problem." He rubbed his chin. "But I thought I should say something just in case. When Dana told me about Sean, I didn't know he was the kid—" Uncle Pete stopped.

Emily hurried her steps toward the house.

"Wait." Uncle Pete took his hat off.

Emily stopped and turned, waiting for him to go on.

"I'm saying this all wrong." Pete yanked his hat back on his head.

"Do you think I have a crush on Sean?" Emily asked. "Is that what you're getting at?"

Pete blushed. "I've heard rumors."

Emily started walking again. Why was everyone so nosy?

"Okay. Good." Pete hurried his step.

Emily shoved her hand in the pocket of the Cornhuskers sweatshirt, right into a folded piece of paper. That's what she'd done with the GED info. She pulled it out and unfolded it. "Hey." She stopped walking. "Uncle Pete, speaking of crushes."

He stopped.

"I have something for you." She held out the paper. "It might be a way to impress Miss Simons." She handed him the paper and then, without waiting for his response, took off jogging toward the house.

AN HOUR LATER, as Charlotte and Bob and the children started out to the truck to leave for church, Pete hurried down the steps from his apartment.

"Are you coming?" Bob asked.

"Nah. I have some research I need to do."

"Research?" Sam yelped. "On what?"

"Just some stuff."

"On the computer?"

Pete nodded.

"Do you even know how to turn it on?" Christopher asked.

"I'll figure it out." Uncle Pete winked at Emily as he strode by.

EMILY STARED AT A STAIN on the Sunday school room's carpet. Beside her, Sam had his head in his hands and his eyes closed, Ashley sat in front of Emily and was totally connecting with Jason, the youth pastor. Everyone laughed a little, except for Emily and Sam.

"I know you've probably heard this story a time or two, but we're going to look at it in a new way. First I'll give a recap."

Emily half-covered her mouth as she yawned. She wished Sean and Rayann would come to church. Rayann laughed when Emily asked her if she was going to go with her mom and then said, "I'd rather sleep."

Jason began telling a story about a man named Jonah who wouldn't do what God told him to do. "He did the opposite of what God asked him," Jason said. Emily yawned again. This time she didn't cover her mouth.

"So Jonah got on the ship and the storm came and Jonah told the sailors to throw him overboard, and he was swallowed by the whale." Emily sat up straight. That part of the story was a little familiar. Maybe Mom had told her the story before. Or maybe she was thinking of Pinocchio. Or had Grandpa read this story during devotions? Sam swayed a little. Emily nudged him. He jerked, and then his eyes flew open and he scowled at Emily.

"Then Jonah prayed this beautiful prayer," Jason said, and began reading from his Bible, "'They that worship worthless idols sacrifice the grace that could be theirs, but I with a song of thanksgiving will sacrifice unto you.'"

Emily tilted her head to the side. She liked the way the words sounded.

"I want us to talk about how we sacrifice God's grace."

Here it came. The moral of the story. Emily yawned again. Ashley had her hand up.

BEFORE CHURCH STARTED, Ashley followed Emily up the stairs to the church.

"Girls, hurry, get out of the cold!" Ashley's mom passed them with two trays of pastries. "Come get a treat in the fellowship hall." Melody's shoes clicked against the concrete as she hurried.

The goodies looked delicious. "Let me help you," Emily said to Melody, taking one of the trays.

"We've been missing you, Emily." Melody's voice nearly sang as she spoke. "Can you come to Ashley's party? Did she tell you that it's a sleepover? Please tell me you can."

Emily froze on the stairs of the church and turned. Ashley bumped into her, nearly upsetting the tray. "You're having a party?" Emily asked. Why hadn't Ashley said anything?

"Ashley, didn't you give Emily her invitation?" Melody asked.

Ashley shook her head. "Not yet."

"Well?"

Ashley opened her Bible and pulled out a small envelope. "Here. It's a week from this coming Friday."

Emily took the invitation and muttered thank you.

"It's just a small party," Ashley said. "Just a few girls."

"Oh." Emily grimaced. She was sure that was Ashley's way of saying she wasn't going to invite Rayann. But that wasn't any surprise. Ashley might have apologized, but that didn't mean that she was going to like Rayann. But that was okay with Emily. Threesomes were so hard to deal with.

Now she needed to decide about Ashley's party. Should she even go?

ON THE WAY HOME from church Grandma asked Sam what the Sunday school lesson was.

He shot Emily a quick look.

"It was on Jonah," Emily answered.

"And the whale?" Christopher asked.

Emily nodded. Sam leaned his head against the window and closed his eyes.

"That was my story too." Christopher unfolded his Sunday school paper. "And grace." He flattened out the paper. The verse Jason read was printed in a big, bold font.

"Grandma, what exactly is grace?" Christopher asked.

"Grace is—" Grandma paused. "Grace is something we don't deserve, such as forgiveness or help or a special blessing."

"Like what?" Christopher asked.

Emily pressed her hand against the cool window of the pickup. What was Rayann doing right now? Maybe she and Sean were going to go into Harding to a movie.

"Well," Grandma turned her head toward the backseat. "Like Grandpa getting to the hospital and getting the medicine he needed."

"Oh." Christopher bounced a little on the seat. Emily put her hand on his leg. He was making her carsick.

"How does God decide?" Christopher kicked the back of the front seat.

"Don't." Emily pressed down on his leg.

"Decide what, sweetie?" Grandma asked.

"Who gets grace and who doesn't?"

"We all get grace," Charlotte said.

"Mom didn't."

Sam opened his eyes. Emily took her hand off of Christopher's leg.

"Oh, sweetie." Grandma twisted further around. "This is really hard to explain. Your mom did get grace. She got heaven. But it feels like we didn't get it, because she died." Grandma paused. "But we experience grace in little ways every day, because we're together, because of God's love, because we love each other."

Christopher was silent for a minute. Emily pressed her nose against the window.

"Grandma?"

Emily wished Christopher would stop talking.

"That was nice that God gave Jonah a do-over."

As Grandpa turned onto Heather Creek Road, Grandma turned toward Emily, but this time she was smiling, just a tad. "Emily, Melody said that Ashley's having a birthday party."

Great. Grandma knew. Emily nodded.

"Well, put it on the calendar as soon as we get home," Grandma said, her voice way too enthusiastic.

Chapter Twenty-Four

Charlotte settled into her chair with the first of the pillowcases in her hand. She picked up her sewing basket and pulled out the skein of green floss. She would start with the palm trees in the nativity scene.

Toby began to bark.

"Someone's here." Christopher called as he jumped up from the sofa and ran into the kitchen.

"It's probably Pastor Nathan." Charlotte stood. "Sam," she called up the stairs. Pastor Nathan's kind voice floated from the kitchen. "So nice to see you." He was shaking Christopher's hand when Charlotte reached them.

She gave the pastor a hug. "Sam will be right down," she said.

"Where should Sam and I study?"

"Here at the table. It should be quiet in here."

Pastor Nathan put a stack of books on the table. "How is Bob feeling?"

"Just fine. He's resting." Charlotte took the pastor's jacket and cap and hung them by the back door. "How about a cup of decaf or a glass of orange juice?" Charlotte asked.

"Juice would be great."

A few minutes later, Charlotte called up the stairs again to Sam. He didn't respond. Finally, she climbed the stairs and knocked on his door. When he didn't answer, she opened the door and found him on his bed with his ear buds securely planted in his head.

"Sam!"

He slowly turned. "What?" He turned off his iPod.

"Pastor Nathan is here."

"*Tonight?*"

Charlotte took a deep breath. "I told you at breakfast and again at dinner that he was coming tonight."

"Oh." He swung his feet over the side of his bed. "I forgot."

Charlotte waited in the hall while Sam dug for his books and notebook in his backpack, and then she followed him down the stairs, stopping at the kitchen door even though she longed to sit down at the table beside Sam to make sure he behaved. Sam waved with one hand, a halfhearted gesture, at the pastor. He held his history book in the other.

Charlotte retreated to the family room and her chair. Sam had been quiet since Saturday. Or had he been quiet since the game on Friday? Charlotte wasn't sure. Christopher sat at the computer doing research for his natural disasters project. Charlotte concentrated on listening to Pastor Nathan and Sam as she picked up her embroidery again.

"How was football today, Sam?" Nathan asked.

"Coach wasn't too upset about us losing."

Sam hadn't said a word on the way home from practice.

A few minutes later the back door opened and closed and Pete greeted Pastor Nathan and Sam. Pete wandered into the family room. "It's too quiet at my place. And cold."

"You should turn on your heat." Charlotte concentrated on lining up her stitches.

"Nah, all I'm going to do is sleep there." Pete leaned against Bob's chair. "So what's with the preacher and Sam?"

"Nathan is helping Sam with history. Actually I think that it's a civics lesson."

"Oh."

"Parliamentary procedure. That sort of thing."

"They still teach that—?" Pete's voice trailed off.

Charlotte nodded.

"That's exactly the sort of thing that made me drop—"

"Pete."

"Mom, no one uses that stuff."

"Bill does, at his city council meetings."

Pete threw up his hands. "My point exactly."

Charlotte shook her head.

Christopher spun around on the desk chair. "Hey, was that storm in Jonah and the Whale a tornado?"

Pete laughed. "It was probably a hurricane. Weren't they on some sea?"

Charlotte nodded.

"Do they have tornadoes over there?" Christopher asked.

"Just sandstorms." Pete patted Christopher's shoulder. "Hey, munchkin, how's that tornado report coming along?"

"Fine," Christopher said. "Actually, not so fine. I need to interview an eyewitness."

"Is this a ploy to get my story? The one Bill was talking about?"

Christopher grinned.

"How about if I tell you tomorrow? Before dinner?"

Christopher frowned. "Can't you tell me now?"

"No. I have other things to do now." Pete shoved his hands into the pockets of his jacket and pulled out a piece of paper. "Mind if I use the upstairs phone?"

"What's wrong with your phone?"

"It's all static-y."

"Since when?"

"I don't know. I noticed it the other night."

"Well, call the phone company."

Pete started walking toward the stairs. There was a phone number written on the paper in his hand, a Harding phone number. "Where do I find the number for the phone company?" he asked.

"On your bill." Charlotte sighed. "And in the front of the phone book. It's on the little desk, in the kitchen."

A half hour later, Pastor Nathan popped into the family room to say good-bye.

"That didn't take very long," Charlotte said to Sam after the pastor left.

Sam leaned against the counter, downing a glass of milk. When he was finished, he burped and then said, "I told you it wouldn't help."

Chapter Twenty-Five

Charlotte poked a knife into the roasting chicken and then set the timer for ten more minutes. Christopher sat at the kitchen table with a notebook, a list of questions, and a sharpened pencil. "When will Pete be here? He said I could interview him."

"Go outside and look for him." Charlotte turned toward the table. Emily had set it and was back upstairs doing homework, and Sam was in the shower.

She heard the sound of a truck rolling over the gravel in the driveway, and Christopher ran to the window. "It's Sean." He slumped back to his chair.

A minute later Sean's Mustang started up, causing the kitchen window to vibrate, just a little. Charlotte watched as he backed his car around and drove away. She couldn't see his face in the dark. Was it awkward for him, not knowing if he should come in or just leave?

The back door swung open a few minutes later.

"Uncle Pete! I've been waiting for you!"

"Hey, munchkin. What's up?"

"The interview, remember? You said you would talk to me about the tornado."

Pete pulled a chair around and sat backward on it. "That's right." Pete caught Charlotte's eye. "And I have to be honest, right?"

Christopher nodded.

The potatoes boiled on the stove, and Charlotte lifted the lid of the pot and speared a potato. The knife slid through.

"When was it that you experienced a tornado?" Christopher read from the notes in front of him.

"It was—" Pete paused. "Let's see, a couple of years after your mom left, I was still in school, a senior, I think, a month before—"

Pete pulled his hat off and scratched his head. "Oh, yeah, it must have been February, an unusually warm day, and Dana and I were—"

"Miss Simons?"

Pete nodded. "That was before she broke up with me, for being a loser."

Charlotte rolled her eyes. Christopher began to write.

"You don't need to write that part down," Pete said.

"What?" Christopher looked up.

"The part about me being a loser."

"Oh." Christopher started erasing, wrinkling the paper.

Charlotte turned off the burner. *Fifteen years ago.* Boy, those were tough years.

"First, I have to tell you that I used to want to be an atmospheric scientist."

"A what?"

"It's a person who studies the weather, that sort of thing."

Christopher started writing faster.

"We were in my pickup."

"Lazarus?" Up popped Christopher's head.

"Yeah, but that was before I called the old boy that. This was before the axle broke, when the truck was just middle age, not a decrepit old man."

"Before the earthquake?" Christopher asked.

Pete nodded.

"And then what happened?"

"I was taking Dana home, on the other side of Bedford, toward Harding. It wasn't late. In fact it was still light." Pete winked. "She was a good student, so she had to get home to study. She wasn't into hanky-panky or anything like that."

Christopher rolled his eyes. "Gross."

"Well, the wind picked up. And then the sky turned green. And we saw this funnel cloud in the distance, over Bell Prairie Road. And I took a sharp right and started chasing it."

Charlotte crossed her arms.

"Okay, time for a disclaimer. I'm making Mom nervous." Pete took off his hat. "Don't ever chase a tornado. It's a stupid thing to do."

Christopher nodded.

"So then Dana started yelling at me to turn around but I kept driving. I'd never been so close, because I'd only seen a few little twisters as a kid out in the field, because whenever there was a warning we were forced down to the basement, in record time." Pete positioned his baseball cap backward on his head. "It was like the tornado was calling my name. And then it wasn't a tornado at all, but a train, a thundering train roaring down on us, and Dana was screaming, and I swerved into a field."

"And then what?"

"It was over."

"That's all?"

"Well, it—actually the winds around the tornado—took a bag of feed and a chest of tools with it, just lifted them from the back of my truck. I never saw them again."

Christopher wrote frantically. The phone rang in the distance; Charlotte assumed Emily would answer it upstairs.

"And then Dana broke up with me the next night—" Pete's voice trailed off.

"Is Pete here?" Emily came running down the stairs. "The phone's for him."

Pete stood, saluted Christopher, and hurried into the family room with the phone.

Who was calling Pete?

"Wow." Christopher's face was flushed.

Charlotte added milk to the potatoes. "Wow is right." She pounded the masher into the pan. "Honestly, Christopher, don't ever do that. I would have taken Pete's truck away if I had known." She had heard bits of the story before but never the whole thing. No wonder Dana got fed up with Pete. Chasing tornadoes while she was screaming. Dropping out of school. He was a case.

Pete came back into the room smiling.

"Who was that?"

"A surprise."

"GRANDPA WAS MISSING IN ACTION for part of the afternoon," Pete said as he passed the potatoes.

"Well, isn't that why you hired a second driver, so I can rest?" Bob took a long drink of water.

"I thought we had a second driver so we could finish harvest and pay the bills."

"Pete." Charlotte passed the green beans to Sam. "He parked his truck down by the old place after lunch, as soon as Sean arrived, and took a nap."

"I was sleepy." Bob cut his pork chop.

Charlotte shook her head at Pete. "Come back to the house and get a decent nap," Charlotte said to her husband. "You'll get a sore neck sleeping in the truck."

"But that would put us behind schedule," Pete said.

"By an hour." Bob lifted his fork to his mouth. "That's all."

"Well, I need you to drive the combine tomorrow."

Bob swallowed his chicken. "Why?"

"I need to go into Harding."

"For?"

"A part to the corn head and to finish up some paperwork."

"Paperwork? What kind of paperwork?"

"After harvest, sometime; it could be a few months before I get into the program. But I'll probably go to Harding a couple of evenings a week, and I need to sign some paperwork now."

Bob put down his fork. "What are you talking about?"

"A high school degree program."

A hoot flew from Sam's mouth. A smile spread across Emily's face. A napkin sailed out of Bob's hand. "A what?"

"I'm going to finish my high school diploma."

"And you're complaining about me taking a nap?" Bob pushed his chair back.

"After I get my diploma, I'm going to take ag classes, at the college." Pete squared his shoulders. "That's my goal."

"You want to go back to school? Now? After all this time?" The wrinkles on Bob's forehead seemed to multiply as he spoke.

"I'm looking for a do-over," Pete said. He smiled at Christopher.

Christopher grinned back.

Charlotte searched her son's face. Was he serious? She would have been overjoyed to hear this news ten or fifteen years ago. And she was happy to hear it now, as long as Pete followed through.

"HOW'S THE REPORT GOING?" Charlotte asked Christopher as she put a basket of towels on the table to fold.

Christopher sat at the table with a tornado book to his nose.

He shrugged.

"I have a story to tell you. Not quite as exciting as Pete's mind you, but you might be able to use it."

Christopher lifted his head.

"It's about a storm—a twister—when I was about your age."

"Really?" Christopher's blue eyes widened. "What time of year was it?"

"It was—" Charlotte set the folded towel on top of the table. "Around this time of year."

He put down the book. "What happened?"

"It took half the roof off my grandparents' house, over east of here."

"Was anyone hurt?"

"No, amazingly. We all got to the basement just in time."

"Were you scared?"

"Not then. I might be now, though," Charlotte answered.

"I wouldn't be." Christopher sat tall.

"How come?" Charlotte tousled his hair.

He shrugged again.

Charlotte folded another towel.

"I've been reminding Grandpa to take his medicine, every morning," Christopher said, closing his book.

"Good." Charlotte sat beside Christopher. "He's okay, Christopher. The new medicines seem to be working."

"He seemed frustrated at dinner, and then quiet," Christopher said.

"Well, you know, Grandpa is a man of few words." Didn't she know it.

She headed down the hall with the towels. Bob stood at the bathroom sink brushing his teeth.

"Are you going to bed?" It was only 8:30 PM.

Bob nodded.

Charlotte followed him into the bedroom. "We never did talk about who should be guardian of the children."

Rosemary had been the guardian for the older kids, but she might not be up for it now.

"Does it matter who the guardian is?" Bob sat down on the edge of the bed and untied his boots.

"I think it does, especially to the kids. Especially since Bill brought it up in front of them."

"He did?"

"Well, Sam was in the room." Charlotte wasn't sure how much Sam talked with Emily about things. Hopefully he hadn't said anything to Christopher.

"I don't know. I just don't want to rush into anything." She paused. "I don't think that Pete would be a bad choice. I think that he would rise to the occasion, and his talk about getting his diploma is encouraging."

Bob smiled, just a little.

"See, I thought deep inside you were pleased that he's considering going back to school."

"Well, I don't know about pleased." Bob took off his other boot.

Charlotte stood. He hadn't been negative about it, and that usually meant he was pleased, at least a little.

Charlotte left the room and told Christopher it was time for bed. She followed him up to his room and checked in on Emily while the boy put his pajamas on. Emily stood by her bedroom window. What was she staring at?

Charlotte stopped beside Emily. "Who's out there?"

Her granddaughter startled. "Uncle Pete and Sean."

"Looks like they got some work done tonight."

"Three loads."

Charlotte raised her eyebrows. "You've been counting."

Emily turned away from the window. "Not really. I just happened to notice."

Chapter Twenty-Six

Sam dropped a pack of stapled papers on the table. "I'm not going to play tonight."

Charlotte dried her hands on a dishcloth. "What are you talking about?" It was the homecoming game. They were all going, including Bill and his family.

"I got my civics test back."

Charlotte picked up the test. *Sixty-seven percent*. "Sam."

He shrugged. "It doesn't matter."

"Really?" Charlotte handed the test to him. It sounded like it mattered.

He slumped into a chair. "I thought I understood all of this."

"Is this what Pastor Nathan helped you with?"

Sam shook his head. "Not the stuff I got wrong; I thought I knew that. He helped me with the stuff I got right."

"Well, why don't you give it another shot? Having Pastor Nathan help you."

Sam shook his head. "I have a test on *Hamlet* in English next Tuesday that I'm not going to pass, and an essay due on Wednesday. I only have a week left until Coach kicks me off the team." He scooted in the chair. "I might as well quit now."

"Well, Sam, whether or not you get your grades up for football, they have to be better if you're going to drive."

Charlotte sat down next to her grandson and put her hand on his shoulder. "We want you to drive. We really do." She was being mostly honest; she did want him to drive, but still the thought frightened her. "But you have to show us that you're responsible."

He nodded. "Grandma." He paused. "Do you think Pastor Nathan would help me again? Maybe this Monday night."

"You can call him and ask."

"Can you call him?"

Charlotte shook her head. "No, but I'll get his number for you."

Sam pulled away. "We should get going," he said.

"So you've decided to play tonight?" Charlotte asked.

Sam nodded.

CHARLOTTE CLAPPED HER HANDS TOGETHER, trying to keep them warm. There was only one quarter of the game left and Bedford was down six to eight.

Bill and Anna sat behind Charlotte, and Christopher and the girls sat in front of her.

"Wouldn't it be cool if a tornado struck the football field?" Christopher said to Jennifer.

Jennifer shook her head.

"Do you know what to do if there's a tornado?" Christopher asked Madison, who sat on the other side of him.

She shook her head.

"Get to the cellar or the basement. Or if you don't have one of those, get in the bathtub, away from a window, and grab towels to cover up with."

"Really?" Madison asked.

Christopher nodded. "If you're outside, lie down in a low spot and cover your head with your arms."

Pete poked Christopher in the back and then said to Madison, "He tells all of us this, all the time. I think he tells Emily every day."

"But she doesn't listen." Christopher pulled his stocking cap off of his head.

Pete shook Christopher's shoulders. "You're like a broken record."

"It could touch down on the goalpost," Christopher continued.

"What about the players?" Madison asked.

"It could pick them up and set them down at the other end of the field." Christopher stood with his hands in the air, waving his cap. "Touchdown! And we'd win!"

"Christopher." Charlotte shook her head.

"May we go sit by Emily?" Jennifer asked.

"Not now." Charlotte glanced back over at her oldest granddaughter, who sat wedged between Rayann and Sean on the edge of the student section. Sean wore his work shirt and jeans and no jacket. "That area is for high school students."

Sam kicked the ball and began running forward quickly. He seemed more comfortable tonight than he had a week ago. Charlotte felt a pang. She wasn't sure if he'd called Pastor Nathan because he wanted to finish out the football season, or because he wanted to drive, but she had a feeling it was the latter.

Sam slipped as a Ridgefield player ran by.

"Boy, it's obvious he's not a football player." Bill said, juggling a bag of popcorn. "I guess they don't tackle in soccer."

Christopher turned his head. "Actually they do tackle. They slide tackle."

"Slide what?" Bill hooted.

Pete turned around. "Knock it off, Bill."

"Pardon?"

"Stop criticizing Sam. He's doing his best."

Charlotte ignored her boys. Those two did always bicker.

A few minutes later, Bill had his revenge. "Hey, Pete, isn't that Dana down there? Your sweetie? Talking to someone else?"

Dana stood to the right of the concession stand, talking to Mr. Santos.

Pete ignored his brother.

"Pete." Bill was louder now.

"Bill." Charlotte leaned back, bumping into Bill's knees. Popcorn spilled onto her coat. "Please." She brushed it away.

Bedford took possession of the ball, but didn't make a first down. Sam punted the ball but it fell short. "Guess they don't punt much in soccer either," Bill said. Pete and Christopher both glared at him.

Charlotte regretted never seeing Sam play soccer. Why hadn't they gone to San Diego to see one of his games? Denise wrote about Sam, her soccer star, over the years. It never entered Charlotte's head that they should think about going out to watch him play, even if they really couldn't have afforded it.

If he had been playing football, Bob would have wanted to make the trip. She shook her head. There was no use in thinking that way.

The band began to play, and the bleachers began to vibrate as the tuba player belted out his notes. The clapping of the students shook the stands. It was the fourth quarter, and Bedford needed to make a move soon.

With only five minutes left in the game, Anna nudged Charlotte. "Look who's headed our way."

Dana was walking up the bleachers toward the Stevenson family.

Charlotte quickly turned to Bill. "Don't you dare say a word."

Bill crumpled his empty popcorn bag and put up both of his hands.

"Stop it," Charlotte hissed.

Anna began to laugh.

"Hi," Dana said, sitting beside Pete just as Ridgefield reached the twenty-yard line.

"Hi." Pete rubbed his chin.

"Hello, Dana." Charlotte reached out her hand and Dana squeezed it. "Do you remember our oldest son, Bill?"

Dana nodded.

"And this is Bill's wife, Anna, and their girls, Jennifer and Madison." Everyone said hello.

"Ridgefield's going for a field goal." Bob sat on the edge of his seat. "Watch." The ball sailed to the right of the goalpost. "Whew." Bob took off his hat and wiped his forehead. "That was a close one."

Charlotte tried not to stare at Dana. Was she just being friendly? Pete said something to her, but Charlotte couldn't hear above the crowd cheering. Dana laughed.

With two minutes left in the game, the score was still eight to six, and Bedford had the ball. On fourth down, Coach sent Sam in to try a field goal. All of the Stevensons stood as Sam secured his helmet and mouthpiece, and he ran onto the field. The ball was at the twenty-five-yard line, but Charlotte had seen him kick from that far at practice. She knew he could do it.

The center snapped the ball to the holder. Sam ran forward. His foot connected with the pigskin, launching it into the air, into the dark, inky sky. The ball twirled. For a second Charlotte lost sight of it against the lights of the field, but then there it was, sailing between the goalposts. The crowd exploded.

"He did it!" Christopher yelled.

Pete slapped Christopher on the back. "That was better than any tornado!"

Charlotte put her hands together in front of her face. Tears stung her eyes. Dana clapped and smiled.

Bob sat down abruptly as he cheered.

"Are you all right?" Charlotte asked, alarmed.

Bob laughed and started clapping. "I lost my balance, that's all."

The student section roared, but Emily, Sean, and Rayann stood calmly clapping. Emily was obviously pleased, but not as overjoyed as Charlotte expected. Was she just acting cool in front of her new friends? Ashley sat behind Emily and waved her arms and yelled.

After the kickoff, Ridgefield tried to come back, working as hard as they could to get the ball to the other end of the field, but the clock ran out after their second down.

Pete whooped and hollered as the final buzzer sounded.

"That's my nephew!" Bill shouted.

After the crowd cleared away, Charlotte and Bob and the rest of the family waited for Sam at the edge of the parking lot. A group of players and cheerleaders stopped a few feet away. "He thinks he's cool," a football player said. Charlotte strained to hear. "If he thinks he's taking Brendan's place next year, he can forget it."

"Yeah," another player said. "For all I care he can go back to California and play soccer."

Charlotte leaned in to listen.

"He did win the game, you guys." The cheerleader giggled as the group headed toward the gym.

Their voices faded. Charlotte took a deep breath.

"Great job!" Bob was slapping Sam on the back.

"Thanks." Sam didn't look as happy as Charlotte expected. Had he heard his teammates?

Bill and Pete congratulated their nephew. Charlotte gave him a hug.

Sam took a step back. "I decided not to go to the dance, Grandma," he said to Charlotte.

"Why?"

Sam shrugged. "I just want to go home." He swung his helmet against his leg.

Emily bumped into her brother. "Hey, hotshot."

He scowled.

She ignored him. "Grandma, I just want to check in before I head over to the dance with Rayann."

"Thank you," Charlotte said. "I'll pick you up at eleven."

"Eleven thirty." Emily's voice was low. "It gets done then."

"I'll be there at eleven." Charlotte rubbed the tips of her fingers up her cheekbone.

Emily frowned.

"You're wearing that to the dance?" Anna asked. Emily wore her Nordstrom jeans and Rayann's Cornhuskers sweatshirt. She had on a pair of white Puma tennis shoes that she'd brought from San Diego but hardly ever wore. She told Charlotte months ago that the shoes had cost ninety dollars.

"What's wrong with this?" Emily frowned.

"Don't you dress up for homecoming? Formals, corsages, the whole bit?" Anna nudged Bill. "Didn't you dress up for homecoming?"

Bill nodded and then turned back to Sam. Sam looked as if he were in pain.

"Are we supposed to dress up?" Emily asked Rayann who stood behind her.

Rayann shook her head. "I polled eight girls. This is what everyone wore last year."

"And what about a date?" Anna asked. "We always had dates."

Charlotte gave Anna a wide-eyed look, slightly shaking her head, but her daughter-in-law didn't catch it. "I think they go in groups now, right?" Charlotte said.

Emily and Rayann both said yes. Sam pulled away from the group and started walking toward the car, alone.

"We'll be there in a minute," Charlotte called after him.

He waved his hand without turning around.

CHARLOTTE WAS SORTING her embroidery floss when the phone rang at 10:20 PM. "Grandma, I have a ride home. You don't have to bother." Of course it was Emily.

"It's no bother. I'm just getting ready to leave the house." Charlotte stood. Bob had gone to bed a half hour earlier.

"But you must be really tired."

"Emily."

"Rayann and Sean can give me a ride. Sean says it's the least he can do. He wants to help you out because you've all been so nice to give him a job."

Charlotte picked up her purse and keys off the desk. "I'm on my way. I'll be there in twenty minutes."

She turned toward the back door and then decided to check on the boys first. Christopher's door was open. She peeked inside. He was asleep, on his back with his arms draped over his head, his mouth open. She tiptoed to his bedside and kissed his forehead.

Sam's door was closed but the light was on. She knocked softly.

"What?"

"Sam." She opened the door. "How are you?"

He sat on his bed with a yearbook spread out in front of him. "Fine." He closed the book.

"I'm going to go get Emily."

"Can I come along and drive?" His voice held a hint of sarcasm.

"Ask me in a few weeks," Charlotte answered, doing her best to respond to his words and not his tone. "I'll be back pretty soon. Grandpa and Christopher are asleep."

CHARLOTTE PULLED ALONGSIDE the school gymnasium as kids poured out the front door. She spotted Ashley with a group of girls and then Rayann, walking out alone. Where was Emily? Charlotte climbed out of her car and scanned the parking lot. Sean's Mustang was in the far corner, away from the other cars. Rayann came up from behind her. "Hi, Mrs. Stevenson. How are you?"

"Rayann." Charlotte smiled at the girl and then craned her neck to look around her. "Have you seen Emily?"

Rayann started to answer when Emily popped out of

Sean's car and waved at Charlotte. "I was just getting my sweatshirt."

"Hi, Mrs. Stevenson," Ashley said as she hurried past Charlotte toward Melody's car. Ashley glanced toward Emily but didn't acknowledge her, as far as Charlotte could tell. Emily stared after her friend for half a second and then turned her attention back to the Mustang. Charlotte waved to Melody and then, despite her weariness, walked quickly toward Emily.

Sean shoved his hands into his pockets as he stopped in the middle of the parking lot. "I just walked Emily out to get her sweatshirt."

"Why are you parked in the corner?" Charlotte crossed her arms.

"I always park over here." He glanced toward his car. "I don't want anyone to scratch my car." He still wore his work clothes.

She was too old, too tired, for homecoming dances and boys and their cars and a granddaughter with a head filled with stars, or maybe straw.

"I'll see you tomorrow, bright and early," Sean said.

Charlotte nodded, trying to remember her manners. "Good-bye Rayann. And Sean."

Emily was silent as Charlotte started the car and pulled out of the parking lot. Charlotte pulled away from the school gymnasium and drove through town.

"Why did you tell me the dance ended at eleven thirty?" she asked once they were on the main road.

"I thought it did, honest." Emily set her seat back a notch. "It's a good thing you came early."

"Emily. I—" What would she have said to Denise? That

Denise had lied? That she was deceitful? Had Emily lied? It looked like it, but Charlotte didn't know that for sure.

What did Emily need? She knew what Emily wanted, but what did she need? Charlotte turned her high beams on as she reached the highway. Emily slumped down in her seat and closed her eyes.

Emily had been abandoned by her father and now her mother was dead. Charlotte glanced at her granddaughter, at her hair that had rebelled against being straightened earlier in the day and was wavy again. Those wonderful, wispy curls. Emily's skin was clear as cream, she had Denise's perfectly sloped nose, and her eyelashes were dark and long with a natural curl.

Charlotte forced her eyes back to the road. How could Emily not know that she was beautiful?

What did Emily see in Sean? He was older and responsible, genuinely so. He was a good, hard worker.

From what Charlotte could tell, it didn't seem that he'd led Emily along in anyway. It seemed to be simply a schoolgirl crush, all Emily's doing.

Charlotte knew that Emily hurt deeply; all three of the children did. She knew Emily cried at night.

Was Emily looking for someone to take care of her? Charlotte prayed for wisdom as they drove silently through the night.

Chapter Twenty-Seven

Charlotte woke to the rooster crowing, but it was still dark. Was it the middle of the night? *No.* The digital numbers on the alarm read 5:30. It was time to get up. She hardly felt like she had slept. Had she worried all night? About Emily? About Sam? About Christopher? About Pete? About Bob's health? She felt for her slippers under the edge of the bed, pulled her nightgown straight, and padded into the bathroom.

Her cold hands warmed under the hot water. The woman in the mirror stared back at her, hair stuck up in the back, like Christopher's did each morning. She had shadows under her eyes. She shifted her head; the shadows moved with it. Six hours of sleep was not enough for a sixty-four-year-old grandmother. Charlotte yawned and patted down her hair.

No use going back to bed now. Bob and Pete would be up in a few minutes wanting breakfast, and Sean would arrive within the hour. She padded back into the bedroom and sat down on the edge of the bed.

Bob stirred. She had wanted to talk to him last night about Emily, but he was fast asleep, of course, when she got home.

"Bob? Are you awake?" Charlotte scooted across the bed, leaning her knee against her husband's thigh.

"No." He turned toward her and opened one eye and then closed it.

"Are you sure?"

"What's up?"

"It's Emily."

Bob yawned. "It's always something."

Charlotte rushed ahead with the story. "She was in Sean's car last night, at the gym, in the far corner of the parking lot." Charlotte braced herself against the headboard. "She said she was getting her sweatshirt."

Bob pushed himself up onto his elbows.

"Do you want me to let Sean go?"

"No. That's not it." Charlotte shook her head. That was Bob, always looking for some easy answer that didn't really address the problem.

"I want to figure out what Emily needs."

"She's a teenage girl. She doesn't know what she needs."

"Exactly." Charlotte searched Bob's face in the dim light. "That's our job. And I know what she needs."

"What?"

She could tell Bob was getting restless. "She needs to know she's loved and that she'll be taken care of." Charlotte stopped. Bob didn't respond. "Could you do something with her today? Take her on an errand maybe? Talk to her?"

Bob swung the covers off her legs. "Oh, Char. What do you want me to do?"

"Talk to her."

"I'm no good at that." He stood, slowly raising himself off the bed.

"Would you try?" Charlotte scooted to the edge of the bed. "Please."

Bob grunted and headed toward the door and then came back to the bed, plopping down beside Charlotte. "I thought things would get easier, you know, now that Denise has been gone—" His voice trailed off. He tried again. "Emily looks so much like her." He took Charlotte's hand.

Charlotte nodded. "I know what you mean."

"I miss her. I miss my little girl."

Charlotte reached for a Kleenex from the box on the nightstand. "That's why we have to talk with Emily, now. I think she'll listen to you more than she does me." Charlotte wiped her eyes.

A little bit of light snuck through the lace curtains. Bob got up and left the room without a word, padding out into the hall to the bathroom. Charlotte wadded up the Kleenex, dropped it in the wastebasket, and walked to the window, pushing aside the heavy curtain. She noticed that the cows congregated near the gate. A single starling flew from the red roof of the barn, and a light came on in Pete's apartment. She wanted to crawl back into her bed and pull her pillow over her head. Instead she turned away from the window and began to dress.

Pete, Bob, and Sean would be harvesting in the north quarter today. Pete thought they would be done with harvest by the end of the coming week.

Charlotte yawned as she pulled on her jeans. She felt exhausted. There was no way she could get everything done that she needed to and be pleasant, not today, not without God's help.

Chapter Twenty-Eight

Emily flipped the hose into the trough and turned on the spigot as a truck turned into the driveway. She jumped onto the fence and leaned forward. The truck rolled, slowly, over the gravel. It was Grandpa. She stepped slowly down from the fence, wrapped her hand around the hose, lifted it, and made lazy figure eights in the tub of water. A heifer with deep brown eyes mooed from a few yards away. How could people eat a creature like that? The heifer headed toward the trough, followed by three cows, all mooing.

"Emily." Grandpa poked his head through the open window of the truck. "I need to drive into town for a part. Want to ride along?"

"No, thanks." She turned back to the trough and slung the water in an S shape.

All of the cows started toward the trough. Toby ran back and forth behind them. Emily turned off the water and wound up the hose quickly. The white-faced calf charged toward her, and the other cows and calves crowded around the trough, bumping into each other as Toby barked. The heifer rubbed against Emily's leg.

"Christopher," she yelled. "Call the dog."

Christopher whistled and Toby took off toward the garden.

Grandpa parked by the house, and then he and Grandma stood by the tailgate talking. Emily started toward the barn to brush Stormy.

"Emily." Grandma stood, shading her eyes. "I need you to go with Grandpa and stop by the store."

"I was going to go take care of Stormy."

"That's okay. Christopher and I will take care of her in a little bit."

What was up? Grandma pulled a piece of paper from her pocket and handed it to Emily. "Here's the list."

Emily looked from Grandma's face to Grandpa's. They looked serious. She shrugged and went inside to get her purse.

Ice cream. Bananas. Fruit leather. Yogurt.

Ten minutes later Emily and Grandpa took off in his pickup. Grandpa turned up the volume to the radio, the same country station that Uncle Pete listened to. The pickup swayed gently as Grandpa drove. Emily relaxed and settled against the seat as her eyes grew heavy. She woke when Grandpa braked for the speed zone on the outskirts of town. "We're here already?" She sat up straight.

Grandpa nodded. "You slept the whole way."

Grandpa parked on the side street by the tractor supply store. She followed him along the sidewalk beside a huge lot with tractors, combines, riding lawnmowers, and a whole lot of other machines that Emily didn't recognize.

Grandpa opened the door of an old brick building for her, and while he talked to the man behind the counter

Emily stared at a display of cleaning supplies. *Cleaning at your fingertips* was the marketing line. That was what Grandpa and Uncle Pete needed, clean fingertips. Emily read closer. The cleansers weren't for hands; they were for carpets and windows and mirrors. She shook her head. Why didn't people around here just buy that stuff at a regular store? Who would think to buy that kind of stuff at a tractor store?

"Ready?" Grandpa held a little brown bag.

"That's all you need?"

He nodded. "A bunch of clamps." He shook the bag, and she followed him out to the pickup.

Grandpa pulled into the parking lot of the grocery store next. "Do you have Grandma's list?"

"Yep." Emily pulled it from her pocket. "Right here."

Grandpa pushed the cart, leaning against it. She had never been grocery shopping with him. He stopped at the popcorn and selected a box, extra buttery.

"That's not on the list, Grandpa."

He winked and tossed in a second box. "But it is corn."

Emily selected a bunch of bananas. Grandpa picked up a pineapple. "How do you know if these are ripe?"

"Smell it."

Grandpa held it to his face and wrinkled his nose. "Hmm." He handed it to her.

"I think it's good." She handed it back. "But it's not on the list."

"Or on my diet. I think they're especially high in sugar."

"And it's probably from really far away, like South America. It's not good for the environment to ship things that far."

Although if it was a ripe mango, Emily would make an exception. And for bananas too. And oranges.

"Well, then," he said and put it back. "Too bad." He pulled a plastic bag from the rack and filled it with apples. "These aren't bad."

At home, back in San Diego, they used to take their own bags, recycled or cloth, to the store. That was better for the environment too.

Emily and Grandpa made their way through the store, strolling up and down each aisle. Emily chose ten containers of yogurt and then two cartons of ice cream.

Grandpa dropped a plastic jar of chunky peanut butter into the cart. "Peanut butter and apples are my new-favorite snack."

"How come?" It didn't seem like something an old man would want for a snack.

"You know."

Emily raised an eyebrow.

Grandpa seemed uncomfortable. "It's good for me."

"Oh. Well in that case—" Emily picked up the peanut butter and read the ingredients. "This has corn syrup in it. It's not good for you, even though it *is* corn." She grinned and put it back and began searching the shelf. There was the brand Mom bought, all-natural, all-peanuts, nothing else added. "Here," she said to Grandpa. "This is much better for you."

"Thanks." He pushed the cart around the corner and then stopped by the chips.

"What are you looking for?"

"Those things Sam likes."

"The jalapeño chips?"

Grandpa nodded.

Emily pointed them out, and Grandpa tossed a bag into the cart.

"What do you want for a treat, little lady?" Grandpa strolled down the bread aisle, eyeing the danishes.

"I'm fine."

"How about if we stop for a milkshake at the Creamery?"

"Can you have a milkshake?" She eyed him skeptically. She didn't want Grandpa to keel over or anything.

Grandpa shook his head. "I'll have coffee, but you can have a milkshake or a soda or anything you want."

Emily headed to the checkout line. "Okay."

GRANDPA STIRRED CREAM into his coffee while Emily took a sip of her chocolate soda. She'd never had one, but ordered it on Grandpa's recommendation. "Delicious," she said, taking the maraschino cherry from the top of the whipped cream and popping it in her mouth.

He smiled. "Your mom always ordered those here."

They sat in silence for a few minutes. Jennie's Creamery was one of Emily's favorite places in Bedford, with its black-and-white-checked floor, red counter, and high-backed booths. Old Coca-Cola advertisements decorated the walls, and an old-fashioned jukebox played music, a tune she didn't recognize, in the corner.

Grandpa cleared his throat, and Emily tilted her head. Was there a purpose to this trip?

"Grandma asked me to talk to you." Grandpa cleared his throat again. "About boys."

Emily felt her cheeks flush and ran her finger along the icy soda glass. She should have known. How much more embarrassing could you get?

"But I can't."

Emily raised her head.

Grandpa chuckled.

Emily stirred her soda. This was *awkward*, as Rayann would say.

Grandpa took another sip of coffee and said, "You can probably guess at what I would say, anyway."

Emily nodded. *Don't date. Don't get pregnant. Basically, don't do what your mom did.* That was Emily's guess.

"So, I won't talk to you about boys." He looked relieved.

She tilted her head. Was this hard for Grandpa? She could empathize.

"But I do want to talk to you about you." He gulped his coffee.

Emily braced herself. Whether he talked to her about boys or about herself, he'd probably say the same thing: *Don't do what your mom did.*

He swallowed and started up again. "You are a beautiful and smart young woman. And I want you to know that Grandma and I—" he paused.

Emily nodded.

"We will do everything we can to help you get through these next four years."

"Thanks." She hoped he was done.

"And one more thing. You need to let us know when and how we can help."

She nodded and took another long drink of her soda so she wouldn't have to answer.

Grandpa shook his head. "You look so much like your mother."

Everyone told her that. "Is that a bad thing, Grandpa?"

"No. No. It's a good thing." His eyes got cloudy. "It just makes me miss her. Makes me wish we would have gone out more, you know, to California."

"Why didn't you?"

Grandpa hesitated, like he needed to ease into what he had to say. "Your mom said we didn't need to. Then we'd get busy on the farm. It's hard for Grandma to fly, 'cuz it makes her ill. It's an altitude thing, but it took a long time to drive." His voice grew quieter with each word.

"I remember you coming out when I was in the first grade."

Grandpa nodded.

"I remember making snickerdoodles with Grandma. I loved the word: snick-er-doo-dles. I'd never heard of them before."

"I just love those cookies." Grandpa smiled. "The little guy was just a baby."

"Christopher was two."

Grandpa stared into his coffee and then raised his wrist. "Look at the time," he said quickly. "I'd better get these clamps back."

On the drive home, fat rain drops splattered against the windshield. Emily closed her eyes and pretended to sleep as her grandfather drove toward home.

Chapter Twenty-Nine

During the night the winds picked up and a bough from the maple tree scraped against the house. Charlotte turned away from Bob and his warmth. Sometime later a knocking woke her completely.

"Grandma! Grandpa!"

Was Christopher ill? She slid her feet to the floor and, without searching for her slippers, stood. The clock read 12:37. The darkness was uncanny. The bough scraped against the window again and something, maybe the shed door, banged against a wall.

The knocking grew louder. She swung open the door and fumbled for the light. Christopher stood in the hallway. "Get up! There's a tornado!"

"Sweetie, what's going on?" The hardwood floor felt cool against Charlotte's feet.

"Did you hear the wind? It's howling." Christopher ran to the stairway and Charlotte followed.

"It's not a tornado," Charlotte said, praying she was right.

Christopher began pounding on Emily's door. She flung it open. "Is the house on fire?"

"No, no. Go back to sleep. Everything's fine." Charlotte put her arm around Christopher. "Let's go downstairs and take a look."

"Charlotte." Bob's deep voice reverberated from the bedroom. "Are you okay?"

"I'm fine," she called back. "Christopher is having a bad dream."

Christopher scowled. "Sort of," Charlotte added.

She led him to the front door and turned on the porch light. The ash trees along the yard swayed, bending low. Charlotte squinted into the night. A branch lay across the driveway. The banging grew louder. "Let's get our shoes on and go out the back door. I'd better find out what that banging is."

Christopher slipped into his tennis shoes without unlacing them, forcing his heel down with a twist. He grabbed a rain jacket that had fallen to the floor and slipped it on.

"Do tornadoes happen at night?" he asked.

"Sometimes, but this is just a wind storm. I'm sure of it." Charlotte pulled her boots onto her feet, grabbed the flashlight, and yanked her corduroy jacket from its peg, pushing her arms through the sleeves.

They tumbled out the backdoor, into a pelting rain that stung their faces. Charlotte flipped her hood onto her head. Christopher ran ahead, and Toby took a tiny step out of her doghouse, shaking.

A bolt of lightning flashed, and Toby retreated. Christopher counted, slowly, to five. The thunder clapped. Toby slinked back onto the grass.

The door at the bottom of the steps to Pete's apartment

swung against the garage, and Lazarus was nowhere to be seen.

Christopher ran to the door and slammed it. Charlotte followed him and pulled hard on the door, making sure the latch had stuck. The wind whipped against their bodies, tugging at their jackets, whirling Charlotte's nightgown around her legs.

"Grandma, look!" Christopher pointed to the field. The gate was wide open. Where were the cows? Charlotte swung the beam of the flashlight into the field. A group huddled down by the fence, but she couldn't tell if any were missing.

She and Christopher hurried to the gate and yanked it closed.

"Did the wind open it?"

"I guess so." Charlotte shone the flashlight toward the herd. The rain had stopped. She swung the beam around, toward the barn and up to the garden. Nothing. A honk startled her. She turned the flashlight toward the road. The white-faced calf ran into the driveway, followed by two other cows, followed by the lights of Lazarus. Toby sprang from her doghouse and took off toward the escapees.

Charlotte followed the dog with the beam of light. "She was too scared of the storm to go after them on her own."

Another bolt of lightning flashed. Toby stopped and whimpered. Pete rolled down his window. "What are you two doing up?"

"Checking on things." Christopher pushed the sleeves of his pajama top up to his elbows.

"Well, help me get the cows in."

Christopher ran ahead to the gate.

"Where have you been?" Charlotte asked as he pulled into the driveway.

"In town."

She frowned. "It's almost one o'clock."

"It's fine, Mom. I stopped at Hannah and Frank's place on the way home. Their old oak tree toppled. I could see it from the road since half their lights were on."

Charlotte's hand flew to her face. "Across the house?"

"It hit the sun porch."

"Is everyone okay?"

Pete nodded. "I told Frank I'd come over tomorrow with the chainsaw." Pete parked his pickup in front of the garage.

Charlotte walked behind the cows as Toby chased them through the gate. Christopher slammed it shut, and Charlotte double-checked the latch.

"I have a piece of wire," Pete called out as he walked toward them, away from the truck. He unwrapped a length from the spool and twisted it securely around the post and a cross bar. "That white-faced calf *is* a regular Houdini, isn't he?"

Christopher nodded and then asked, "Did you see any funnel clouds? Out there on the road?"

"Nah, but there are lots of limbs down."

They called out their good-nights, and Charlotte and Christopher headed back to the house while Pete went to his apartment above the shed. She sat down beside Christopher and tucked him into bed.

"That was scary." Christopher wiggled under his covers. "The wind can do a lot, huh? Slam doors. Open gates. Knock down trees. I guess I might not be very brave during a tornado."

"Christopher, you were brave. Being brave doesn't mean not being afraid; it means doing what you need to do, even when you are afraid."

Christopher inched toward her and reached for her hand.

"Have you heard of Christina Rossetti?" Charlotte asked.

"Who?"

"She's an author."

Christopher shook his head.

"I memorized this when I was your age." Charlotte took a breath and then continued,

> *Who has seen the wind?*
> *Neither I nor you:*
> *But when the leaves hang trembling*
> *The wind is passing thro'.*
>
> *Who has seen the wind?*
> *Neither you nor I:*
> *But when the trees bow down their heads*
> *The wind is passing by.*

"That's nice, Grandma." Christopher's eyes drooped. "Thank you."

Charlotte patted his shoulder. "Good night; sweet dreams."

He was asleep before she turned off his light.

She walked slowly down the stairs and then slipped back into bed, snuggling against Bob, placing her cold feet against his flannel pajamas.

"Everything all right?" he muttered.

"Everything's just fine," she answered.

Chapter Thirty

Sunday after dinner, Christopher sat at the table, working on his tornado project. "Did you know that some tornados have multivortexes?"

"I had no idea." Charlotte put the leftover roast into the fridge. She tried to keep from showing that she was getting a little tired of tornadoes.

"Grandpa didn't seem too crazy about those sugar-free brownies." Christopher kicked his foot against the table leg. "But I thought they were pretty good."

Charlotte covered the brownies with Saran Wrap. Christopher had eaten two, and everyone else had had a bite.

"What's key lime pie?"

Charlotte put the brownies on the table. Maybe if they were in plain sight, they'd disappear. She sat down beside Christopher. "Key lime pie is one of Grandpa's favorite desserts." Bob had mentioned how nice it would be to have key lime pie after he tried to swallow his bite of the brownie.

"When are you going to make one?"

"Sometime." She brushed brownie crumbs into her hand. "I need to find a low-sugar recipe." She stood, flung the crumbs into the garbage, and looked out the window. Bob lumbered from the garage toward the shed. "I don't think I have any in my cookbooks."

"You can look online."

Charlotte turned back to Christopher. "Pardon?"

"Online. That's where Mom used to get most of her recipes."

"Oh." Charlotte hadn't thought of that.

"You just Google in what you want to make and it pops up with recipes."

"What a good idea." She patted Christopher's shoulder. "May I have another brownie?"

"Of course."

"You like those?" Sam stood in the doorway making a face.

Charlotte ignored the comment. "Are you done with the computer?" she asked.

Sam shrugged. "For now." He turned toward Christopher. "Want to go kick the ball around, Chris?"

"I'll come out in a few minutes." Christopher put his nose back in his book.

Pete sashayed in the back door as Sam headed out. *A revolving door.* That was what Charlotte needed.

"I'm headed over to Hannah's to work on the tree." He grabbed a brownie, wiggling it out from under the wrap. "Do you think you could bring Sam and Christopher over in an hour or two? They can help stack the wood."

Christopher jumped off his chair. "That sounds like fun."

"Sure." Charlotte urged Pete to take a second brownie.

A minute later she sat down at the computer. She was tempted to ask Christopher to help her, but resisted. Where was the online button? She scanned the bottom of the screen. There it was. She clicked and then began typing in the letters for key lime in the search bar. K–E—*Oh dear.*

The words *Kevin Slater* popped into the box. Charlotte jumped. Which one of the kids was trying to find their dad?

SAM AND CHRISTOPHER clambered from the car, racing toward Pete.

"Hold your horses," Pete called out, turning off the chainsaw. "We need to have a safety lesson first."

Charlotte turned off the ignition, and Hannah waved from the porch.

The two met halfway. "Would you like to go for a walk?" Charlotte asked.

"That's just what I need." Hannah hugged her friend.

Charlotte had worn her Nikes on purpose, hoping Hannah would be up for walking.

"Unless you have things to do?"

"Like what? Stack wood?" Hannah swept her arm toward the tree, Pete, and the boys. "I've got your kin to do that."

Charlotte tied her sweatshirt around her waist. The late afternoon was still warm.

"I can't tell you enough how much I appreciate Pete stopping last night and then coming over this afternoon," Hannah said as they started down the road. "This kind of thing is getting to be too much for Frank."

Charlotte nodded. She couldn't explain to Hannah, not really, how much it meant to her that Pete saw that their neighbors needed help and offered it without any prodding.

She and Hannah chatted as they walked along the rutted road, deeper into the Carters' property, alongside the harvested fields of soybeans on one side and corn on the other.

They slowed at the creek. The water ran quickly around a boulder.

"Is something bothering you?" Hannah asked.

"No." Charlotte sighed. "Well, yes."

"What is it?"

Charlotte told Hannah about Kevin's name popping up on the computer screen. "It startled me far more than I thought it should."

"Of course it would startle you."

"I'm sure it was Emily." Charlotte continued. "Maybe she thinks that living with her dad—wherever he is—would be better. You know, he would let her do whatever she wanted, go out with a senior, stay out late. All of that."

"But you don't know it was Emily."

Charlotte thought for a moment. She knew, for sure, that it wasn't Christopher. It could be Sam. *Still*. "Emily's my first guess."

"Did you ask her?"

Charlotte shook her head. "Do you think I should?"

"You could ask her." Hannah frowned. "But you know, just because she Googled her dad it doesn't mean that she's trying to find him. Maybe she just wanted to see if there was any info on him online."

That seemed unlikely to Charlotte, but then Bill had said the other night that sometimes he searched for articles about himself on the Internet. A sigh escaped her lips. "But what if Emily has contacted Kevin? What if he shows up, ready to take the kids?"

"Denise left the kids to you and Bob. It was in her will, right?" Hannah asked, her voice full of concern.

"Yes." But Charlotte wondered about Denise's will. It was done off a Web site. Would it hold up in court? She wasn't about to ask Bill, not now anyway. She could just imagine the complicated advice he would offer. "I'm just afraid that if Kevin wanted the kids that a judge would give them to him. He's their father."

Actually, she didn't know if Kevin had ever given up his parental rights to the kids. Denise had never said and Charlotte couldn't find any proof when she went through Denise's paperwork.

"But he abandoned them." Hannah's voice was firm.

Charlotte pulled her sweatshirt from her waist and wrestled it over her head.

"Charlotte, the kids aren't going anywhere," Hannah said. "No one's heard from Kevin in years. He didn't pay child support."

Charlotte wanted to believe her friend, but the worry knot tightened in her stomach.

"Have you prayed about this?" Hannah asked.

Charlotte shook her head.

"May I pray?"

Charlotte let out a long breath, and Hannah prayed that God would keep the children safe with Charlotte and Bob, and that God would show Charlotte if she should talk with Emily. "Amen."

"Amen," Charlotte repeated.

They walked a few moments in silence and then turned back toward the Carters' home. Christopher and Sam, arms full of wood, worked beside their uncle.

"Charlotte," Hannah slowed. "Do you ever pray for Kevin?"

Charlotte stopped. Did she pray for Kevin? *No.* In fact, she hadn't prayed for him, not once, in at least eight years.

Chapter Thirty-One

"Grandma, that lime pie was really good." Christopher licked his lips as he spun around on the computer chair.

"Key lime pie." It had been good, a dessert the whole family enjoyed. She expected that by bedtime it would all be gone.

"Right." He stopped spinning and put his hands on the keyboard.

The sewing box sat center-stage on the coffee table. Charlotte pulled out the green floss to continue the palm trees on Sam's pillowcase.

Laughter from the kitchen, from Sam and Pastor Nathan, filled the house. Emily was at Rayann's studying algebra, and Sean and Pete were still out in the fields. Charlotte would buzz into town later for Emily.

Sam had put out his books before Pastor Nathan arrived, and he had reported after practice that his history teacher was allowing everyone to retake the test and try to bump their grades up. Apparently the entire class had done poorly.

"Listen to this." Christopher spun around on the chair

with a paper in his hand. "Most tornadoes rotate counterclockwise in the northern hemisphere and clockwise south of the equator."

"My goodness," Charlotte said. "I had no idea." She fastened the hoop onto the pillowcase and bent over the taut fabric.

"What are you doing, Grandma?"

"Working on a project."

Christopher turned back to the computer. A moment later a tornado clip on YouTube came onto the screen. Christopher turned up the volume, and the eerie scream of the recorded wind made Charlotte shiver. "Would you turn it down, please?"

Christopher complied.

The front door opened and Pete called out, "Mom."

"I'm in here."

Pete hurried into the family room. "Can you drive the last load? Sean had to go home."

"Why?" Charlotte set the pillowcase in her lap.

"Something's up with his grandfather, and his sister is upset."

"Oh no." Charlotte bit her lip. "Emily is over there."

"Oh." Pete shoved his hands into his pockets. "Well, can you drive? I really want to get this load to the elevator."

Charlotte placed the pillowcase in her sewing basket. "I need to go get Emily." Why had she allowed Emily to study with Rayann tonight?

"Where's Dad?"

"Out at the shop." Charlotte stood. "I'll go get him."

"I can drive." Pastor Nathan stood in the doorway to the kitchen.

Pete spun around.

"I drove for the Bells last fall when they were in a dilemma. I can drive tonight." Pete looked from Nathan's face to Charlotte's and let out a long breath.

"Nah, Pastor." Pete took a couple of steps toward Nathan. "Sam needs your help more than I do." Pete winked. "I'll go get Dad."

If Charlotte hurried, maybe she could get there soon after Sean. She just hoped Sig Campbell was all right.

Chapter Thirty-Two

Emily sat at the table in Rayann's dining room alone and stared at her open algebra book. She and Rayann had spent an hour doing nothing—well, except gossiping about people. Rayann said quadratic equations were really easy, that they didn't really need to study, but now Rayann was helping her mom.

Emily looked at the first homework problem. She'd copied it from Rayann's paper, but she didn't understand it all. When she did it on her own, she kept getting the wrong answer. She walked into the kitchen. The clock said *7:20*. Grandma would arrive in forty minutes.

She reworked the first problem again and then looked at the quadratic formula again.

A door down the hall opened and closed and then opened again. "Rayann." Margaret's voice carried down the hall. "I'll figure this out, but we can't go on like this."

Another door closed. A couple of minutes later the door opened again and footsteps fell on the hardwood floor of the hallway.

"Hey." Rayann sat down next to Emily. Her face was red and puffy.

"How are things?" Emily put down her pencil.

"Grandfather's okay. He fell. Mom wanted to call for help, but I told her we could do it." Rayann pushed her algebra book away. "We finally managed to transfer him from the floor to his wheelchair."

"I could have helped," Emily said.

Rayann shook her head. "He would have been embarrassed. I called Sean though, right at first. But now we don't need him."

"That must have been scary."

"He's been falling a lot. Mom said we can't keep doing this. We need to get him into a care facility. Mom had already looked into one back in Lincoln."

"Lincoln?"

"Bummer, huh?" Rayann shook her head.

"But I thought you wanted to go back home."

Rayann turned toward the hall. "I did. But now I'm not so sure. I like it here."

Emily nodded.

"And besides, I don't have any friends like you back home." Rayann frowned.

Emily smiled, just a little, thinking about Bekka, Nat, and Steph back in San Diego. And then, to her surprise, she thought of Ashley, too, but then she shook her head. She would miss Rayann; she'd never had a friend quite like her. "When will you go?" she asked.

"Oh, I don't know. Not for a while. Mom said there are long lists at all the places she's called."

Emily let out a sigh of relief. She couldn't imagine Bedford without Rayann and Sean.

"If harvest is done by Friday, Mom wants to take Grandfather to the family cabin on Lake Monroe. A sort of last hurrah for him." Rayann slumped against the back of the chair just as Sean burst through the front door and started for the hall, but when he saw Rayann he stopped.

"We got him up," she said, shaking her head.

"Does Mom need help?"

Rayann shook her head.

Sean said hi to Emily and sat down at the table. His clothes were dusty, and he had a streak of dirt across his forehead.

"We're going back to Lincoln." Rayann sat up straight.

"When?" A smile spread across Sean's face.

She shrugged. "As soon as Mom finds a place for Grandfather."

"Wow." Sean clasped his hands behind his neck.

"I need to go ask Mom something." Rayann headed back down the hallway.

A current of emotions raced through Emily. Her breathing felt shallow. The moths in her stomach started to fling themselves about. She tried to smile at Sean. He was happy to move back to Lincoln.

She'd been hoping that maybe by summer, when she was fifteen, he would see her for who she was, that Grandma, too, would recognize her maturity. That she wasn't like other girls her age. That had been her fantasy, that Sean would go off to college and wait for her, and they would date when he came back to Bedford. That by the time she was ready for college, maybe—

"Hey, do you want some iced tea?" Sean called from the kitchen.

"No, thanks," Emily said, her voice squeaking a little.

He returned with a full glass. "I'll miss Heather Creek Farm the most," he said. "Your family has been really good to me."

Emily nodded. She couldn't think of anything to say but his words comforted her. They were the best thing she'd heard all night. Maybe—

There was a commotion, and Emily turned toward it. Margaret wheeled Mr. Campbell up the hall. He was even thinner than the last time she saw him. He smiled at Emily and softly said, "Hello."

Margaret pushed her father into the TV room, and Sean downed his iced tea. Where was Rayann? Emily craned her neck, looking for her friend. Margaret headed back down the hall, and right away Emily could hear Rayann and her mother talking again. Then the doorbell rang.

"It's probably Grandma." Emily stacked her book and notebook, but before she was done, Sean had opened the door.

Grandma stood under the porch light, her pink work shirt wrinkled, and her hair sticking up in the back. "Sean, is everything all right?" Grandma asked.

"I think so. Grandfather fell, but Rayann and Mom got him into his wheelchair." Sean invited Grandma inside.

"We'd better get going, Emily." She didn't look suspicious for a change, or angry that Sean and Emily were alone.

"I just want to tell Rayann good-bye." Emily felt shaky. What would Bedford be like without Rayann and Sean? But maybe it would be months before they left.

"I'll go tell her that you're leaving," Sean said.

Emily wiggled into her denim jacket and picked up her

books, and then Grandma noticed Mr. Campbell by the TV and went in to say hello.

Rayann came out of the bedroom to say good-bye, but Sean stayed back with their mother. "I'll see you tomorrow. Don't worry about the test; you'll do fine." Rayann said.

Emily shrugged. She didn't care about the test anymore.

Grandma said good-bye and led the way down the steps, and Emily sunk into the front seat of the car.

"What's the matter, Em?" Grandma started the car.

"They're leaving."

"Leaving?"

"Going back to Lincoln."

"What about Mr. Campbell?"

"They're taking him to a care facility or something."

Grandma put her hand on Emily's knee. "I'm sorry."

Just then the front door of the Campbell house swung open and Margaret hurried out while Rayann stood on the porch. Margaret headed around the car, to Grandma's window, and Grandma opened it.

Margaret was out of breath and mascara smudged the loose skin under her red eyes. "Charlotte, I'm glad you hadn't left yet." She leaned toward Grandma. "I want to take everyone, including Sean, if harvest is done, to our cabin on Lake Monroe this weekend. It might be Dad's last trip there." She looked so sad. "And Rayann came up with a great idea. We would like Emily to come along. We have to take two cars, because of all of Dad's stuff. We'll have plenty of room. She's been such a good friend to both Rayann and Sean."

Grandma took a deep breath.

"Please, Grandma." Emily leaned forward.

"Let me think about it." Grandma ignored Emily.

"Of course. We'll leave Friday after school. Just call and let us know."

Grandma and Margaret chatted more about her father, who had end-stage emphysema.

"Life can change so quickly," Margaret said.

Grandma nodded. "I know."

Margaret patted Grandma's hand. "Of course you do; you and Emily both know better than anyone."

Emily stopped herself from thinking about Mom. She didn't want to go there, not tonight. Instead, she practically held her breath, trying not to beg Grandma. Finally she couldn't any longer and once they left Bedford behind, she wailed, "Puh-lease?"

"I know you want to go, but I'm not sure, Emily," Grandma said as they pulled onto the road. "Margaret is so busy taking care of her dad that there doesn't seem to be much supervision."

Emily felt a rush of anxiety. She might never see Sean—and Rayann—again. "Grandma. Rayann has been my best friend here."

"What about Ashley?"

Emily turned her head toward the dark night and shrugged.

"Emily, friendships have to be nurtured. You can't just flick them around depending on your mood or who moves to town."

Emily didn't answer.

Grandma began to drum the steering wheel with the tips of her fingers. "It seems like there's something else going on this weekend."

Emily started to say no, but stopped.

"Ashley's party," Grandma slapped her hand against the vinyl ring. "That's what's on the calendar."

Emily groaned out loud. She couldn't believe that Ashley was going to mess up her opportunity to have one last chance to spend time with Sean and Rayann. "She doesn't even want me to go to the party," Emily moaned. "She only asked me because her mom made her."

"Emily, how can you say that? Ashley is your best friend in Bedford."

"Was."

"Pardon?" Grandma said.

"She *was* my best friend." Emily crossed her arms and sank low in the seat.

Chapter Thirty-Three

Pastor Nathan came out the back door as Charlotte turned off the ignition. Emily flew out of the car, past Pastor Nathan with a slight wave of her hand, and into the house.

Charlotte stepped from the car. "How did it go?"

"Better." He glanced over his shoulder. "Much better than Emily's evening, I'm afraid."

"She's had some upsetting news." Charlotte clutched her purse, not sure how much to say.

Nathan waited.

"Her new friends, Rayann and Sean—"

Pastor Nathan nodded. "Margaret's children."

"Yes. They're moving back to Lincoln."

"I was afraid it had come to that," he said. "I can see that Emily would be sad. She has a lot in common with them, more than with most of the other students."

Charlotte nodded. She could see that too.

"We all want to be understood. There's no one who understands us better than someone who can empathize, even partly."

Charlotte nodded again. "Well, thank you for helping Sam. I can't tell you how much we appreciate it."

They said their good-byes and Charlotte hurried into the house. She hoped Christopher was getting ready for bed.

"What's wrong with Emily?" Pete sat at the kitchen table, eating the last piece of key lime pie.

Charlotte hung up her coat. "Why? Did she say something?"

"That you're mean."

"That I'm mean?" Charlotte crossed her arms.

"Mom, don't take it personally. Remember, she's a teenager." A crumb tumbled from Pete's mouth to his chin, and he wiped it away with his thumb.

Charlotte sat down at the table. "Where's Christopher?"

"Brushing his teeth." Pete took another bite. "I read his tornado report."

"You did?" Charlotte wanted to chuckle. Maybe Pete *was* serious about starting school again.

"He's a smart kid." Pete licked his lips.

"I worry that he doesn't have friends, though."

"He has us."

"Still, don't you think he should have friends his age?"

Pete opened the refrigerator and slung the milk pitcher onto the counter. "I think you should leave Christopher alone." Pete poured a glass of milk. "Do you want one?"

Charlotte started to say no, but then changed her mind. A glass of cold milk sounded good.

Pete sat back at the table, sliding a glass in front of Charlotte. "Don't expect Chris to be like anyone but himself. Okay? I know what that's like, and it's not fun."

"What do you mean?" Charlotte jerked her head up.

"You wanted me to be a mini Bill, to get straight A's and play football."

"No, I didn't, Pete."

"Mom, you and Dad were both so disappointed in me. You always were, so eventually I quit trying."

Charlotte frowned and took a sip of milk. What was Pete talking about?

"After Denise left, you expected me to be perfect, to redeem the family."

"No, Pete, I never expected that of you." Her throat thickened and her hand shook a little as she put her glass down. Where had he gotten that? She had been embarrassed, yes, that Denise left, pregnant. And she had been disappointed that Pete dropped out of high school. Well, devastated was more like it. But she hadn't been disappointed in Pete before that.

Or had she? Well, she hadn't meant to show him anyway.

"Just don't do the same thing to Christopher, okay? He has too much going for him." Pete drained his milk. "And good luck with Emily." He stood. "I'm off to bed."

"Wait." Charlotte put out her hand and touched his arm, trying to shake his words. "Pete, no matter what, I love you and I'm proud of you. I never meant to give you any other impression."

"Don't worry about it." Pete patted her hand, but the gesture felt forced to Charlotte.

She sighed and changed the subject. "I should let you know that Sean's family is going back to Lincoln."

"When?"

"They're not sure."

"Whew." Pete patted his chest. "You had me scared. You

sounded like they were leaving first thing in the morning." Pete headed to the back door. "That's too bad, though. I like Sean. He's a nice kid."

Charlotte rinsed her glass, and Pete's, and placed them in the dishwasher. Had they really favored Bill? Had Pete felt their disappointment that intensely?

She took a deep breath and let it out slowly. She couldn't start replaying the past again. She didn't have the energy for it, not now, not when she needed to cope with the present.

She climbed the stairs slowly. Bob was already in bed. Christopher was already asleep. Emily's door was open, a crack. Charlotte knocked. Maybe she wasn't as upset as she seemed. "Emily?" Charlotte called out. The room was empty.

Charlotte checked the living room, family room, and kitchen. Still no Emily. She trudged back up the stairs. Emily's room was still empty. Charlotte stopped at Sam's door. "Have you seen Emily?" she asked as she knocked.

"She's in here."

Charlotte opened the door. Emily slouched on the end of Sam's bed, clutching a photo.

"I wondered where you were." Charlotte stepped into the room.

"We're just talking." Emily stood and held the framed photo away from herself. It was the picture of the four of them, of Denise and the kids.

"Grandma, Ashley would understand. Totally."

Charlotte shook her head. From what she saw of Emily and Ashley's current relationship, she didn't think Ashley would understand at all.

"Then I'll make up an excuse. I'll say that I need to help you with something, something church related."

Was Emily serious? "Emily, that would be a lie. We don't lie."

Emily crossed her arms and then dashed away, taking the photo with her.

CHARLOTTE WENT BACK OUT into the hallway, leaving Sam alone in his room, and as she passed Emily's closed door she heard a muffled voice. She went down the stairs to the safety of the family room. The photo of Denise and her was facedown on the end table; Charlotte left it that way, too sad to turn it over. Tears stung her eyes as she picked up her embroidery.

A few minutes later Emily passed by in the hall.

"Em," Charlotte called out.

Her granddaughter stopped in the doorway.

"I was looking up a recipe the other day, on Google. And your dad's name popped up in the search field."

Charlotte might as well ask since Emily was already upset. Things couldn't get worse.

"Dad's name?"

Charlotte nodded. "I wondered if you were looking for information on him."

"Grandma." Emily's voice rose. "I have no idea what you're talking about." She flounced down the hall toward the kitchen.

Chapter Thirty-Four

"Charlotte!" Rosemary called out from behind the counter of Fabric and Fun. "What a nice surprise."

"How are you?" Charlotte plopped her purse on the counter.

"I need another cup of coffee." Rosemary threw her hands in the air. "Want one?"

"Sure." Charlotte followed her sister-in-law into the small office at the back of the shop.

"Sit."

Charlotte settled onto a padded chair next to a table.

Rosemary took a mug with a sunflower painted on the front from the cupboard, put it on the kitchenette counter top, and poured coffee for Charlotte. Then she refilled her own, a bright orange mug, and added creamer.

"How goes it?" Rosemary sank down onto a chair.

"Oh, you know." Charlotte felt as if all she did was complain—to Hannah, to Rosemary, to Melody. No wonder Bob didn't want to listen to her for long.

"How's Sam feeling about football? How are his grades?"

"He has two tests today, so we'll see."

"Are they going to win Thursday night and make it to the playoffs?"

Charlotte shrugged. Sam thought they could win.

"How's Emily?" Rosemary clapped her hands together. "Ashley's party is this Friday, right?"

Charlotte nodded.

"Melody was telling me all about it. Emily should have a blast," Rosemary said.

Charlotte leaned toward her sister-in-law. "She wants to go to the Campbells' cabin with Margaret and her kids; they invited her."

"But she already told Ashley she'd go to the party?"

"Yes."

"That's too bad."

"Not really. I don't want her going to the cabin."

Rosemary took a long sip of coffee. "I see your point. But Margaret and the kids are going back to Lincoln."

"I know. But Margaret doesn't supervise the kids. She's so busy taking care of her dad that they're alone a lot." Charlotte took a sip of coffee.

Rosemary pulled another thread off of her apron, this time a purple one. "Oh dear. I hadn't thought about that. It's been so long since I've been around teenagers—I forgot about all of that." Rosemary grinned. "Believe me, I don't envy you one bit."

"You're no help." Charlotte cradled the cup in her hand. "To complicate matters, Emily and Ashley haven't been getting along."

"I thought they were best friends."

"I thought so too." The warm mug brought a little bit of comfort to Charlotte, but not much.

"Well, you know how these things go for girls. It's day to day. Wait until next week. Everything will be fine."

Charlotte smiled. She hoped so.

She caught Rosemary up on Sam and Christopher; then Rosemary asked about Bob.

"He's doing great. He's still tired, but the blood clot has completely dissolved. He had another ultrasound yesterday." Charlotte glanced at her watch. "Speaking of, I should get going. Bob and Pete are going to be ready for lunch in an hour."

They headed to the front of the store. "Oh." Charlotte stopped. "I almost forgot what I came in for."

"What can I help you find?" Rosemary asked.

"I need more green thread, for those palm fronds. I think Lightning stole a couple of skeins."

"A pack cat, huh?" Rosemary laughed.

As Charlotte rummaged in her purse for a five-dollar bill, she lamented about how little time she had for embroidering. "I don't know how I'll get the pillowcases done by Christmas."

"I could help you."

Charlotte handed Rosemary the money. She was tempted. "Thanks. Who knows, I might take you up on it. Let's see how it goes." But she wouldn't feel the same if Rosemary helped. She wanted to make something for each of the children. She should have done it years ago.

"Oh dear." Charlotte stopped.

"What? What's wrong?"

"I should get a gift for Ashley. For her party." Charlotte glanced around the shop. "Maybe a candle."

"How about a gift certificate? She comes in here all the time." Rosemary pulled out a piece of paper and an envelope.

"Perfect," Charlotte said.

CHARLOTTE HAD BEEN COLD when she went to bed and she had piled one too many blankets on top of herself. Now she was sweating. She turned toward the clock. 1:17. Bob turned his head toward her. He sucked in some air and then exhaled, loudly. She hoped he wasn't working up to a full-strength guttural snoring session.

She flipped the extra blanket to the end of the bed and turned onto her side. Toby began to bark. She was too tired to herd cattle tonight. The dog barked again. It was probably just a raccoon. Raccoons, kids, and a barking dog. Emily and the cabin. Escaping cows. Sam and football and school and driving. Christopher and his lack of friends. The horses, Pete and his degree completion program...and Dana. Harvest. Bob and his health. A barking dog. Bill and his wish to be made the children's guardian. She was too tired to think about any of it.

What was Toby barking about?

Charlotte forced herself from bed, snatched her bathrobe off the footboard, kicked her feet into her slippers, and opened the curtain a sliver. There was Toby, sitting in the driveway, barking at the harvest moon high above the barn.

She made her way down the hall, bleary eyed but too awake to go back to sleep. She called to Toby out the back door and the dog slinked back to her doghouse.

Charlotte stopped in the kitchen for a glass of water and then headed to the family room, tripping over Christopher's Spider-man backpack. Too tired to move it, she stepped over it, pulled the afghan from the couch, wound it around her shoulders, and then sank into the couch.

Charlotte couldn't see the row of family photos that hung on the wall, but each one was vivid in her mind. Bob's parents on their wedding day, his mother in a stylish 1940s suit. Bob and Charlotte on their wedding day, Charlotte's hair teased in a near beehive, Bob wearing a white tux jacket and black trousers. There was a photo of Anna and Bill taken at the Lincoln Country Club. Anna wore a designer gown and a tiara, and Bill stood behind her, his arms wrapped around her waist. Charlotte had removed Denise and Kevin's wedding photo eight years ago.

Charlotte stood and made her way to the hall. It was the picture next to her wedding photo that she wanted to see now. It was of her children when they were still kids. She squinted, trying to see clearly in the dim light. Denise looked straight at the camera, her pale blonde hair braided with thin strands floating around her pixie face. Her eyes laughed. Pete looked as if he were in on Denise's joke. Bill sat up straight, a near frown on his face.

Charlotte took the photo off its hook and stood in the middle of the hall. Charlotte had been mortified when she found out Denise was pregnant, but she'd never expected her to leave.

Bedford kids stuck around, usually. They stayed in Nebraska or at least in the Midwest. All the time Denise was growing up, Charlotte had taken it for granted that her only daughter would marry a local boy, raise horses and children, go to her parents' church, celebrate holidays and birthdays, and do all the things that grown daughters did with their mothers. She never expected Bill to stick around. In fact she was surprised when he took the job in River Bend. She expected he would end up in Lincoln or Omaha or Chicago or even Washington. But she assumed Denise, and Pete, would stay close.

Denise was eighteen, technically an adult, and she made her own decision, but Charlotte had felt abandoned by Denise all those years ago when she took off with Kevin.

She lightly touched her finger to Denise's six-year-old image. "My sweet baby girl," she said. "How I miss you." In the end it wasn't the pregnancy that was the hardest thing. Sure, she was embarrassed, but she got over that eventually. It was losing Denise and then not seeing her grandchildren. Not knowing her grandchildren, that was what had broken her heart.

"What are you doing?"

Charlotte startled. "Oh." The picture frame slipped from her hand and crashed to the floor with a clinking of glass. "Oh," she said again, her hand flying against her chest.

Emily, with her hair in braids, hurried to her grandmother's side and picked up the photo.

"Careful, the—"

"It's broken," Emily said, carefully holding two pieces of glass and the frame.

"Why are you up, sweetie?" Charlotte asked.

"I couldn't sleep."

"Want a glass of milk?"

"Sure." Emily followed Charlotte into the kitchen and slid the glass in the garbage. "May I have it warm, please? That's how Mom used to fix it for me, when I couldn't sleep."

"That's how I used to fix it for your mom." Charlotte set the frame on the counter.

Emily opened the refrigerator and reached for the milk.

"I was thinking about going to the cabin. That's why I couldn't sleep."

Charlotte nodded and pulled a pan from the cupboard.

"If it wasn't for Ashley's party, would you let me go?" Emily stood in the middle of the kitchen, the pitcher in her hand.

"If it wasn't for Ashley's party, maybe I would offer to go along to help Margaret."

"Grandma!" Emily wailed.

Charlotte tensed at her granddaughter's voice. "What?"

"You don't trust me." Emily slung the milk onto the counter. "I'm not my mom, if that's what you're worried about."

Charlotte's stomach fell. "No, Emily, that's not it."

"Then what is it?"

Charlotte turned toward her granddaughter. "I don't want your life to move too quickly, for your teenage years to get ahead of you, that's all."

"Whatever." Emily slumped onto a chair.

How had they gotten here? A few minutes ago everything was fine.

"I don't know why you're so worried about Sean. It's not like he likes me."

Charlotte poured the milk into the pan and turned on the burner. "But you like him, right?"

Emily stood, scraping the chair on the linoleum. "Don't worry about heating any milk for me. I'm going back to bed."

Chapter Thirty-Five

Charlotte pushed up the sleeves of her raggedy pink shirt and slipped on her work gloves. Today was the day to burn the leaves. She had put it off long enough. The afternoon was cool with no wind. Toby ran around in circles, chasing her tail, as Charlotte scooped up leaves and dumped them in the burning barrel. The dog darted toward the road and then back.

"Five more minutes," she said, as if Toby could understand. "Then Christopher will be home."

Sean turned the truck into the driveway and rolled down his window. "Mr. Stevenson sent me up for a snack. He said he needs some juice and a cookie."

"Where is he?" Charlotte started toward the truck, clapping the leaves off of her gloves.

"Down at the old place."

"Why didn't he come?"

Sean shrugged. Charlotte headed to the house and grabbed a box of apple juice from the pantry and a cookie.

Sean stood beside the truck and climbed back in as she approached. "Thank you," he said.

"No. Thank *you*." Charlotte handed him the juice. "I'll come down as soon as the kids get off the bus."

Toby began barking in earnest. "I know, girl, I know. It's time." Charlotte followed the dog down the driveway to the road, keeping back from the dust kicked up by the truck. She would need to keep the hose close by when she burned the leaves.

Christopher flew down the steps of the bus and buried his head in Toby's fur. He lifted his head. "Grandma, I'm going to finish my report today, and turn it in early."

"Good for you."

"Come on, Emily," the bus driver yelled. "Hurry it up."

Charlotte squinted.

Emily emerged and took each step one at a time. Charlotte wanted a chance to talk with her about last night, but not with Christopher around.

"Grandma, would you read my report?" Christopher threw a stick for Toby. "After I print it out."

"Sure. First I'm going to check on Grandpa, though. Want to go with me?"

Christopher shook his head.

After she read his report she needed to start dinner and then go get Sam. Maybe she wasn't going to burn leaves today.

She started her Ford Focus, backed out of the driveway, and headed down the highway to the field turnoff. She met Bob coming out of the gate.

He rolled down the window of his truck. "I'm fine," he said. "Yes, I checked," he said, answering her question before she could ask it. "I was at sixty-two. That's why I sent Sean to the house. I was loading on the go." Annoyed, he pulled out onto the highway.

Charlotte turned around and zipped the other way. *Kids and men. And cows and dogs. Who could predict what any of them would do?*

Back at the house, Christopher presented his report to her to read. The report was good. It started with the worst tornado outbreak in US history. In 1974, in less than twenty-four hours, 148 tornadoes touched down in a nine-hundred-square-mile area from Ontario, Canada, to Mississippi, and from North Carolina to Tennessee. The winds reached 318 miles per hour and 330 people were killed.

Charlotte remembered the event, but still, the statistics startled her. Life could never be predicted. Everything could change in an instant.

She read on. He had included Charlotte and Pete's tornado stories and concluded the report by saying that he hoped to see a tornado someday and when he went to college, he wanted to study atmospheric science.

"Your report is great, Christopher. I learned a lot," Charlotte said, smiling at her grandson. He really was a good student.

Christopher beamed.

Charlotte hoped Sam was doing as well with his studies. Tomorrow was the last game, and Coach said he would check with Sam's teachers and then decide tomorrow if he could play or not.

The sound of the front door opening and closing caught Charlotte's attention. Was Bob back? *No.* No, he would come in the back door. Charlotte headed to the front door and walked out onto the porch. Emily stood by Sean's car, next to Sean.

"Hello, Mrs. Stevenson." He waved. "We stopped early today. Pete said to tell you that he and Mr. Stevenson will be done soon, after they work on the combine."

Charlotte nodded. She stood still for a moment, watching, then went back in the house. She started scrubbing the frying pan, gazing out the window to keep them in her sight.

A moment later Emily came inside, and Charlotte heard Sean's car on the driveway gravel. Emily took an orange from the fruit bowl and began to peel it as she sat down at the table. "Sorry about last night," she said.

Charlotte turned from the sink. "Thank you. Apology accepted."

"I was tired." Emily arranged the peels in a neat stack. "It's not as big a deal as I thought. Sean said they'll be here at least a few more months."

Charlotte kept scrubbing.

Chapter Thirty-Six

Thursday after school Charlotte asked Sam if he would be able to play in the game that night, the last game of the season.

He shrugged. "Coach said he hadn't heard back from all of my teachers. He's going to call."

"What do you think?" Charlotte asked.

He shrugged again as he peeled a banana. "I don't know and I don't really care. It's not like I have a future in football."

Christopher slid into the room and asked Charlotte for a cough drop.

"Are you coughing?" she asked.

"My throat hurts."

She felt his forehead. It didn't feel warm. She pulled the bag of cough drops from the pantry and handed him one.

"What about next year?" she asked Sam. "Don't you want to play then?"

"Brendan will be back on the team."

"But you're better than he is. Everyone says so," Christopher said, and then sneezed on his way back to the family room, not waiting for Sam's response.

Sam turned toward Charlotte. "But Brendan's been playing since he was a little kid." Sam tossed the peel into the trash can. "He deserves it."

Charlotte nodded. She was proud of Sam for being considerate of Brendan, but she still wished that he wanted to play next year. He needed something to keep him motivated.

Sam walked to the fridge and poured himself a glass of milk.

"Do you care about driving, Sam?" Charlotte asked.

He shrugged again, but this time he didn't look as convincing. He downed the milk in one long drink.

As Sam put his glass in the sink, the phone rang.

"Could be your coach." Charlotte sat down at the table. She nodded to the phone.

Sam walked slowly to pick it up, but it stopped ringing before he got there.

"It must be for Emily." Charlotte said. "If not, she'll be yelling down here in just a second." Charlotte paused. It had to have been for Emily. "Go tell her to be quick," Charlotte said to Sam. "Tell her that you're expecting a call."

A few minutes later the phone rang again. This time it was Rosemary calling to see if Sam was going to play in the game. "I'll call you back." Charlotte quickly hung up the phone.

Christopher sneezed again. Charlotte could sense the force of it, all the way in the family room.

"Are you getting a cold?" Charlotte called to him.

"Allergies," he called back.

Charlotte didn't contradict him, but that seemed highly unlikely. The phone rang a third time just as Sam sat down at the table.

Charlotte answered it. "He can play," Coach said without preamble. "He just squeezed by in history. Seems he retook a test or something. That paid off. Tell him to keep working. In fact, tell him to work a little harder."

Charlotte gave Sam a thumbs up and thanked the coach. A half smile began to spread across Sam's face, but then he turned his head and got up and left the room.

Charlotte heard another sneeze. Lightning curled beside Christopher on the couch, purring loudly.

Charlotte felt Christopher's forehead again as he stroked the cat's thick coat.

"I'm fine," Christopher said. "Just a little tired."

Now he felt a little warm.

She fetched the thermometer from the bathroom and took his temperature. It was 100.0. Not too high, but he could be coming down with something. "Sorry, sweetie. It looks like we'll have to miss the football game tonight."

Emily hurried down the stairs with her homework notebook and stopped in the family room doorway.

"Grandma," Christopher wailed.

"What's going on?" Emily asked.

After Charlotte explained that she was afraid Christopher was coming down with a virus, Emily quickly answered, "I'll stay home with him. I don't want to go to the game anyway."

"But it might be the last one."

Emily shrugged. "So?"

That might work. Charlotte would like to see Sam play, but she wasn't sure about leaving Emily in charge.

Sam stopped behind his sister. "What's the matter? Isn't Sean going to the game? Is Uncle Pete working him too long?"

Emily elbowed him. "I have no idea if Sean is going to the game," she said, rolling her eyes.

"Too bad that Rayann isn't." Sam elbowed her back.

"Who says Rayann isn't?" Emily asked.

"Well, is she?"

"Sam," Charlotte chided.

"No," Emily answered.

"You don't do anything without Rayann and Sean." Sam bumped into Emily again.

Emily slammed him with her hip. "I'm going to—"

"That's enough." The conversation was all that Charlotte needed to decide she would stay home, because otherwise she'd be worrying about Emily inviting Sean into the house after he was done for the evening with only her sick little brother as a chaperone.

"Emily, you do what you want as far as the game, but I'm planning to stay home with Christopher."

Emily spun around. "I'm going back upstairs to do my homework. I can't think down here." She stomped up the stairs.

"How will I get to the game?" Sam asked.

"I'll take you, and Grandpa can bring you home." Charlotte patted Christopher on the head. "I think Bill is going to the game, and Rosemary is for sure." In fact, she needed to call Rosemary. "Go make a sandwich to eat in the car," Charlotte instructed Sam. They had to get going if they wanted to make it on time. "And I'll get you some Tylenol," she said to Christopher.

Chapter Thirty-Seven

"I really, really wish you could come to the cabin with us," Rayann said over the phone.

"Me too." Emily sat on her bed, cross-legged, and wrote her name in flowery letters on the college-ruled paper that she was supposed to be rewriting her English essay on.

"Aren't I more important than Ashley's party?" Rayann whined. "Seriously, your grandma is being harsh. Don't you think?"

"Kind of."

"I mean, she knows that I'm going to be moving soon. You can go to Ashley's party next year and the year after that." Rayann sighed. "And the year after that."

"I know." Emily started to add, again, that she really did want to go to the cabin, when Rayann interrupted to say that she had to get off the phone.

"Mom wants to talk to me," she said.

Emily pushed the off button and dropped the phone onto her bed. She wrote out the first sentence of her essay: *The consumption of animal fat and protein increases body weight and the risk of osteoporosis, heart disease, cancer, high blood pressure, dementia, and diabetes.* She read what she wrote. It was kind of wordy.

Diabetes. That was probably why Grandpa had it. He ate a lot of meat. And now he had high blood pressure too.

What should she write next? She wasn't sure, so she wrote: *Sean Matthews*. Then she wrote it again, this time with curly cues, then with block letters, then in all lowercase letters. Then ten more times as fast as she could.

She heard a knock on her door and quickly folded the sheet of paper several times and stuffed it into her pants pocket. There was another knock. "Come in."

It was Christopher, with a dictionary in his hands.

"Where's Grandma?" Emily asked. She'd heard Grandma come back from dropping Sam off a while ago.

"Milking." He sat on the edge of her bed. "I was looking up *guardian*."

"Guardian? Why?"

"Uncle Bill picked up Grandpa to go to the game. I was in the family room, but I heard him ask Grandpa if he'd made up his mind, if Uncle Bill and Aunt Anna were going to be our guardians."

"Uncle Bill is just talking. He wants Grandma and Grandpa to redo their wills." Emily closed her notebook. At least that's what Bill had been talking about last time they were over.

"I looked up *guardian* in the dictionary." He opened it up to where his thumb was and read: "Someone who takes responsibility for someone else, such as an orphan."

Emily nodded.

"Are we orphans, Em?"

"No. We have Grandma and Grandpa."

"Then why does Bill want to be our guardian?"

"In case something happens to Grandma and Grandpa."

"Oh." He closed the dictionary. "Would we have to move to River Bend? To that house with all the white carpet?"

"I don't know. Don't think about it, okay, Christopher?"

"Couldn't we just live here with Pete?"

"I don't know."

"Couldn't we—"

"Would you stop?" Emily jumped from the bed.

The phone trilled and Emily snatched it off the bedspread. "Scram," she hissed at Christopher and then answered the cordless phone she'd left on her dresser.

"Emily." It was Rayann.

She waved good-bye to Christopher. Why was he just standing there?

"Are you absolutely sure you can't go with us to the cabin?"

Christopher turned slowly and left her room.

"Because listen to this." Rayann whimpered. "Mom said that we might have to move back to Lincoln as early as next week. They might have a place at the care center after all."

Next week! "You're kidding." Emily crossed to the window and pulled back the curtain. Sean's car was still parked by the shop.

"No. Mom's going to call in the morning to find out for sure. So ask your Grandma one more time, okay?"

"Sure," Emily said, even though she knew there was no way that Grandma would change her mind.

"And if that doesn't work, I have a brilliant plan." Rayann talked quickly. She would tell Sean, after school, that Emily could go to the cabin after all, but they needed to pick her up. Emily would have her overnight bag packed to go to

Ashley's party so all she needed to do was sneak out of the house with the bag and meet them down at the road.

"And then what?" Emily asked.

"Well, you'll leave your grandma a note. I'll help you write it. We'll include the number to the cabin and tell your grandma to call my mom."

Emily sighed. *Yikes.*

"So it will be late by the time they talk. Then you say, when my mother explains that there has been a miscommunication, 'But Grandma said I could come.' My mom is so tired she won't deal with it. She'll just tell your grandma that we'll bring you home on Sunday."

"And then I'll be grounded until, I'm like, twenty-nine."

"But it won't matter," Rayann shot back, "because Sean and I won't be around. You won't have anyone to do anything with anyway."

Emily plopped down on the bed. Rayann was right about that. Ashley hadn't talked to her for days, not since a rumor got started that Emily planned to ditch Ashley's party.

"So is it a deal?"

"No." Emily pursed her lips.

"Oh, come on. How about if we have to go back to Lincoln next week? Promise me you'll do it if that happens?"

Emily didn't answer.

"Your grandmother would probably regret being so strict if you sneak off like that. Grown-ups are always second guessing themselves."

"I've got to go, Rayann." Emily walked back to the window. The truck turned into the driveway. "I've got to write my essay."

She hit the off button and tossed the phone onto her

bed. Emily took out the piece of paper in her pocket with Sean's name and folded it again, over and over until it was a tiny square. Sean parked the truck and walked to his Mustang, quickly glancing toward the house.

She stepped back from the window. Was he looking for her? She peeked around the curtain. He stood by his car and stretched. *Yes*, he was looking at her window. She smiled. He had said that he would miss Heather Creek Farm the most when they moved back to Lincoln.

The Mustang sped away. Emily sat back down on her bed and took out a fresh sheet of paper.

A half hour later, when she heard cars in the driveway again, Emily started down the stairs and walked into the kitchen at the same time as Grandpa, Bill, Pete, and Sam.

"I was willing to move here for the sake of the children, but Anna said we have to think about our own children first," Bill said.

"You're like a broken record." Pete looked as serious as Emily had ever seen him. "All you can talk about is Mom and Dad's will and who gets the kids and who gets the farm. Christopher must have gotten his obsessive gene from you."

"Pete." Grandma hurried in from the family room. "*Shhh.*"

"Don't shush me." He swept his hat off his head. "I'm sick of Bill acting like a politician with us. This is our life, not a bunch of documents." Pete turned and saw Emily. "Oh, hi there." He blushed and pulled his hat back on his head.

Grandpa headed toward the hall.

"Bob," Grandma's voice was tense. "Where are you going?"

"To bed."

"Who won?" Emily asked Sam as he started through the kitchen, carrying his sports bag.

"They did." He kept on going, straight to the stairs with an odd smile on his face.

Emily stepped toward the sink and started putting away the pots in the draining rack. She wanted to look busy. Maybe they would keep talking.

"I'll do those later." Grandma said, coming up behind her. "Go on up to bed."

"Listen, Bill," Uncle Pete said. "You're really bugging me. Quit bringing this up."

"Bill," Grandma's voice was soft. "Dad and I said we needed to talk about this. We'll meet with our lawyer here in town when we're ready." Then Grandma turned toward her. "Emily, now."

Emily nodded but reached for a baking sheet.

"Okay, okay." Bill's voice rose. "I'm just trying to make things easier for all of us. You would not believe the number of people who wait until it's too late."

Grandma poked her head into the hallway. "Emily," she said. "Go to bed."

"I can't believe they lost," Bill said as Emily walked slowly toward the staircase. "And I still can't believe Sam doesn't care that they're not going to the playoffs. What's wrong with that kid?"

A FEW MINUTES LATER there was another knock on Emily's door. It was Grandma. Emily sat up and put her head in her hands.

"What's wrong?" Grandma said, sitting down on the bed beside her. "Is it the stuff Bill was talking about?"

Emily shook her head. "Rayann might move next week."

"Oh, sweetie." Charlotte smoothed Emily's hair.

Emily leaned her head against her grandmother's shoulder, breathing in her grandmother's clean scent. "Please may I go to their cabin? I want to hang out with Rayann before they move."

Grandma drew Emily close and remained silent.

"Please?"

"I know you're disappointed, Emily." Grandma took a deep breath and let it out slowly. "I've already decided, sweetie. The change of circumstances doesn't change my decision."

Emily sprang to her feet. "That's so unfair."

Grandma stood slowly. Her face was drawn and pale. "We can talk about this more later, maybe tomorrow, Emily. But my decision stands." She walked to the door. "Good night. I love you." She closed the door gently.

She loves me. Emily spun away. *Yeah, right.* Now, thanks to Grandma, she had to decide whether to go along with Rayann's plan. "Please don't let them go back to Lincoln next week," she whispered. "Please let them stay here longer."

Chapter Thirty-Eight

Friday morning, Charlotte settled into her chair and cradled a cup of coffee. She yawned. *Lord*, she prayed, *I'm tired.* She placed her Bible on her lap and thumbed through it. She had been reading in Galatians. As she flipped through the pages her Bible fell open to the last two pages of the book of 2 Corinthians, and her eyes landed on a verse she had underlined years ago: "My grace is sufficient for you, for my power is made perfect in weakness."

Lord, she prayed, *I don't have the answers for these kids and I know I can't control them. You don't even want me to. You want them to learn to trust you. You want Emily to learn . . .* She closed her eyes. *Emily.* She worried about her the most. *Lord*, she whispered, *I trust you. I know your grace is sufficient for me. I know it's sufficient for Emily—*

"Grandma?"

Charlotte jerked as she opened her eyes and coffee sloshed over the side of her mug onto her Bible. She dabbed at it with her sleeve. There was Emily in the doorway again.

"Grandma, what are you doing?"

"Praying."

"For?"

Charlotte placed the coffee on the end table. "For you."

"Oh." Emily stepped back and wrinkled her nose.

"Why are you up so early?"

"I didn't get a shower last night, and I want to straighten my hair." She held her clothes and makeup in her hands. "I'm going to use the downstairs bathroom. Sam's up already."

"Hurry, Grandpa will need in there soon." Charlotte read further in the passage and prayed through her list, finishing with, *Okay, God, it's your day. You're in control.* She heard Bob's heavy footsteps in the hall and headed into the kitchen as Pete passed the window and burst through the backdoor. "Is Dad up yet?"

"Yep."

"Good." Pete rubbed his hands together. "Because we have a butt-load of work to do."

"Pete, don't be crass."

"What?" He looked around. "Are any of the kids up?"

"Sam's in the upstairs shower." Charlotte pulled a pan from the cupboard for Bob's oatmeal. "And Emily's in the downstairs shower."

"Well, I learned the phrase from her." Pete turned toward the coffeemaker. "She's always saying that she has a buttload of homework."

Charlotte shook her head. Maybe Bill was right. Maybe Pete wouldn't be the best influence, but she was tired of thinking about the guardian issue. God was going to provide for the kids one way or the other, but if they didn't want Bill to be the guardian, they'd better decide soon. If something did happen and they hadn't appointed one, Bill would win by default. She was sure of it.

Bob made his way into the kitchen and pecked Charlotte on the cheek. "Is it an oatmeal day or an eggs day?"

"Oatmeal," she answered.

Bob snapped his fingers. "I thought so."

"Hurry." Pete poured more cream into his coffee. "We have a lot of work to do, and no Sean this afternoon."

"No Sean?" Charlotte asked.

"No, he and his family are going to their cabin. He needed to help his mom get ready."

"We'd better write him a check for the rest of his hours then." Bob sat down at the table. "No reason to make him wait."

"I'll talk to Emily about it." Pete sat at the table. "She can give him the message."

Charlotte turned the burner under the oatmeal off and headed to the barn to milk Trudy. She'd let Christopher sleep awhile longer. He didn't have a fever last night when he went to bed, but the extra rest would do him good.

CHARLOTTE CHECKED HER WATCH as she left the grocery store. 1:30. She had plenty of time to stop by Mel's for a cup of coffee. Charlotte paused. Margaret Matthews walked out of Kepler's Pharmacy down the street but hurried straight to her car. Charlotte reminded herself to call her to say good-bye before the Matthewses left town.

Clouds crowded the southern horizon. Charlotte hoped it wouldn't rain on Ashley's party, as she climbed from the car, her purse over her shoulder, and pushed through the door into the café.

Ginny waved from behind the counter. "I'll be right

with you." Charlotte nodded and took a seat at the counter. Melody was nowhere to be seen. She settled in for a long wait.

A new set of paintings hung on the wall. Rayann's signature was at the bottom of one with a white cat sitting on a blue wingback chair next to a fireplace. The fireplace was only partly in the painting though, and the flames looked as if they were about to light the chair on fire. Charlotte stepped back. Rayann was one of those teenage girls who acted as if she had everything figured out, as if she assumed she knew more about the world than the adults around her, but Charlotte didn't see that in the painting. It seemed to communicate vulnerability, not confidence.

"Hi, Charlotte!" Melody came in from the kitchen, drying her hands on a tea towel. "What can I get for you?"

"A coffee." Charlotte paused. "And a piece of pie, I think. Peach."

"Oh, Charlotte, our pie isn't nearly as good as yours." Melody chuckled. "Are you sure you want a piece?"

Charlotte laughed. "You're putting me on, right, Melody?"

Melody shook her head. "No, I'm serious." She poured the coffee and then served the pie onto a plate. "Four-seventy-five," she said.

Charlotte handed her a five.

"That's too bad that Emily can't make it to the party tonight." Melody handed Charlotte the change. "We'll miss her."

"Pardon?" Charlotte nearly choked on her pie.

"Ashley called at lunchtime and said Emily can't make it," Melody said, her smile fading. "She said she has a family obligation."

Charlotte shook her head. "There must be a misunderstanding." What was Melody talking about? "Emily is definitely going to Ashley's party."

"Oh, good. Ashley must have heard wrong, that's all." She handed Charlotte a fork. "I'm so relieved. We'd hate to have Emily miss the party, and I think it will be good for the girls to spend some time together. You know."

Charlotte nodded. She did know, and she appreciated Melody for not discussing it anymore with her. The girls needed to sort things out.

"I'll go ahead and make a cheese pizza too, besides the pepperoni," Melody said.

After Melody left to wait on another customer, Charlotte felt an uneasiness build inside of her. Was Emily up to something? Had she really told Ashley she had a family obligation? What if it wasn't a misunderstanding?

Charlotte took a bite of the pie. It wasn't bad. She sipped the coffee.

Melody returned and sat with her for a few minutes and they talked about Sam and the football season ending. Then Melody asked, "When does he plan to get a car?"

"I'm not sure, but he's doing better in his classes. If he keeps up his grades, he can get his license."

"Mel," Ginny called from the kitchen. "I need you to take a look at the pastries. They look a little dark."

"Excuse me." Melody stood, a little resentfully it seemed.

Charlotte finished the pie. She sat and stared at Rayann's painting. Bob and Charlotte had forbidden Denise to see Kevin, absolutely forbidden her, all those years ago. Did it drive her to him more? And then she got pregnant, and there was nothing more Charlotte could do. Charlotte sighed. After all these years, she really didn't know what they should have done differently. *God*, she prayed, *once was enough. I never asked for a do-over, not on this.* She drank the last sip of coffee. *I just want to raise these kids, not repeat my mistakes.*

CHARLOTTE STOOD ON THE PORCH and pulled her sweater tight. The clouds that had started in the south were now scuttling across the sky. She would burn the leaves tomorrow. Based on the way the clouds were moving, it looked like the wind would soon pick up. Maybe rain was on the way. She hoped that Bob and Pete would finish Jimmy's quarter before the storm hit.

She stepped down the stairs and stopped on the walkway, craning her neck. A flock of geese flew above, appearing over the roof of the house and then continuing on, over the stubble of the field. Their shadows floated effortlessly over the ground toward the willows at the far end of the field. They flew silently, over the creek, away from the farm, encouraging each other to keep moving forward.

"Toby, it's time," Charlotte called out. The dog came around the side of the house, wagging her tail. "Let's go meet that bus."

Sometimes Charlotte had a hard time remembering what she used to do before the children came to live with them. She quilted some. Cleaned more. Spent more time on her Bible study. Embroidered often enough to finish a project. She cooked less, and sometimes she even took a nap. What a luxury. She laughed out loud. What a waste of time.

She walked to the end of the driveway just as the yellow

bus crested the hill and rolled toward her. The bus stopped and Emily, Christopher, and Sam climbed down. The driver waved to her and the bus rumbled on. Charlotte stood facing town, knowing what was coming next: the Mustang. In just a moment the car came into view and Sean waved from the front seat. Rayann smiled from the passenger seat as Sean rolled down his window.

"I came for my check," Sean said. "Pete told Emily I should."

"It's ready for you in the house."

Emily hurried ahead of the car and then waited at the back door while Sean parked. Sam slipped inside, probably headed to his room, and Christopher handed his backpack to Charlotte and then took off toward the barn with the dog.

"Come on in," Charlotte said. Emily, then Rayann and then Sean followed her into the house and stopped in the kitchen. "Tell me. When are you headed back to Lincoln?"

"Early next week," Sean answered. "Mom found a place for Grandfather in a care center."

No wonder Emily looked so dejected. "Well, I hope you can stop by next week and tell Pete and Mr. Stevenson good-bye before you go. I know they've really appreciated your work."

Sean nodded.

"Emily, offer Rayann and Sean a snack. I'll be right back." She'd written the check that morning, and now she picked up the envelope from the basket on the top shelf of the desk and took it back to Sean.

"Thank you," he said, brushing chocolate chip cookie crumbs from his hand. "I really appreciate all that your family has done for me."

"You're welcome."

Emily pulled Rayann's Cornhuskers sweatshirt out of her book bag. "You'd better take this."

"Keep it, please."

A horn honked. Rayann turned her head.

"It's the mailman," Emily explained. "He honks after he goes by. Christopher will get it."

Sean turned toward his sister. "We'd better get home and finish helping Mom." Sean walked ahead to the car.

"Sean's actually feeling okay about going back to Lincoln," Rayann said to Emily as Charlotte followed them out the door. "He was talking to Whitney again last night."

"Whitney?" Charlotte said.

"His girlfriend?" Emily sounded as dejected as she looked. Charlotte cringed.

"Hey, Sean." Rayann quickened her step. "Did you call Whitney this afternoon? Are you two getting back together?"

He turned. "Knock it off, Rayann."

"What?"

"Could you just stop? Just this once?"

Rayann threw her hands in the air. "What's with you?"

Emily hugged Rayann good-bye as Charlotte stood to the side of the driveway, waiting for Christopher to come back from the mailbox.

"Have fun at Ashley's party," Rayann called out in a chipper voice as she climbed into the car.

"Have fun at the cabin." Emily didn't sound as enthusiastic as Rayann.

As they drove off, Emily hurried toward the chicken coop. Well, that was something. She remembered to do her chores before going to Ashley's party. Charlotte hadn't even reminded her.

Christopher waved as Sean drove by and then started running toward Charlotte. "Sam got a letter," he said, breathlessly. "It's from Sacramento."

"Really."

Christopher handed it to her. "Who do you think it's from?"

There was no name above the return address. "I don't know." Had it been Sam who was searching for Kevin? She had been so sure it was Emily.

Christopher handed her the rest of the mail and then ran back outside. Two bills and *The Bedford Leader*. She held them in the opposite hand as Sam's letter.

The envelope from Sacramento felt like lead. She kept walking. Would Kevin show up in a few days, ready to take the children? She trudged up the stairs and knocked on Sam's door. "You have a letter," she said.

The door flew open, and she handed it to him, not wanting to let it go.

"Thanks," he said. She waited.

"Thanks, Grandma." He snatched it from her and closed his door.

Had she expected him to open it right then? To show it to her? "You're welcome," she answered, and started down the stairs.

Chapter Thirty-Nine

Emily stood in the middle of the chicken yard scowling at the rooster. "Leave. Me. Alone." She stomped toward him. He backed off.

The giddiness of moths flying willy-nilly in her stomach had given way to a hollow feeling. *Whitney.* Sean's girlfriend had a name. A really cool name.

The chickens began to congregate around Emily, pecking at her shoes. She hurried into the coop and fed them. Emily began to feel sick to her stomach. It didn't help that the afternoon had grown muggy. She pushed her hair away from her face and watered the chickens.

Why had she agreed to Rayann's plan? It was a stupid idea, so stupid that they kept needing to adjust it. Like with Sean driving out to the farm to pick up his check. That set them back forty minutes. Now, as soon as they got back to their house Rayann would pretend that Emily had called to say she could go to the cabin, and then Rayann would have to talk Sean into driving back out to the farm. It was a ridiculous plan, and she knew Grandma and Mrs. Matthews would be upset and so would Sean once he found out they had tricked him.

Rayann was so sure of herself, but Emily wasn't. She wasn't at all sure this was a good idea.

Emily fled the coop and stopped in the middle of the chicken yard. She took the note out of her pocket. Rayann had told her what to write:

Grandma,
　Please understand how important it is for me to go with Rayann this weekend. She's the best friend I've ever had.

That wasn't really true. She liked Rayann, she really did, but she was too controlling. Bekka had been her best friend in San Diego. And Ashley had been her best friend in Bedford. Until Rayann moved to town.

　We're just going to the cabin. Call Mrs. Matthews this evening. We should be there sometime after 7:30. She'll tell you that everything is okay.
*　　　　　　　　　　Love,*
*　　　　　　　　　　Emily*

At the bottom of the page was the phone number for the cabin.

Emily shoved the note into her jacket and then dug the tiny square of paper from deep in the pocket of her jeans. She opened it up. *Sean Matthews. Sean Matthews. Sean Matthews.* Over and over and over. He had been nice to her, but that was it. He'd probably been relieved that Rayann had a friend, and relieved that he had a job.

She tore the paper in half and then stomped her foot again. She tore the paper in fourths. Two chickens squawked and fluttered about, and she tore the paper into eighths and then sixteenths. Three more picked their way out of the coop as she tore the pieces of paper into tiny, tiny pieces that began to fall to the ground. The chickens gathered around, their beaks poking at the pieces of paper. Emily threw the rest of the scraps into the air and stepped away from the cloud of confetti. The chickens pecked and pecked, breaking the paper into bite-size papers and gobbled them up. Soon only a few remained.

A minute later Emily ran up the stairs of the farmhouse, snatching the phone off the table on the landing. She dialed Rayann's number, but no one answered. They'd already left to come back to the farm! Sweating, Emily stripped off her jacket, and the note to Grandma fell from the pocket to the floor. She picked it up, wadded it into a ball, flung it on the bed, and grabbed her overnight bag from her dresser. She flung it over her shoulder and slammed out her bedroom door, colliding with Sam.

"Whoa." He put out his hand and steadied Emily as she stumbled. "Where are you headed?"

Emily clutched her bag to her chest. "Ashley's party."

"I need to talk with you about something first." He waved an envelope in front of her face.

"I don't have time." She pushed past him.

"It's about Dad." He pulled a piece of paper from the envelope. "I found some addresses after Bill said he wanted to be our guardian."

"What?" Emily stopped short and snatched the letter, reading it quickly.

"It's from Dad's old landlord." She slumped against the hall wall.

Emily read out loud. "Kevin Slater moved from this apartment complex several years ago and left no forwarding address." That was all. How could Sam even know if the guy *was* their dad?

"It could be *any* Kevin Slater," she said.

Sam took the paper back. "Still. It could be a start."

"Whatever." Emily walked to the landing. Christopher stood on the fence with his finger in the air as Toby barked, running back and forth along the field. "I've got to go." Emily started down the stairs. Finding their father was the last thing she wanted to think about right then.

SHE DROPPED HER BAG on the porch and sailed across the lawn to the driveway. Christopher spotted her and started yelling. The wind had picked up and Christopher's unzipped sweatshirt flew behind him. Leaves from Grandma's pile swirled around. Christopher began to run after her.

"Emily!" he yelled again.

She turned. "Go to the house! I'll be right back."

He kept running. "There's a storm coming!"

"I just have to *do* something, then Grandma is going to drive me to Ashley's." That's all she needed, for Christopher to see Sean's car.

Christopher stopped. Toby whined and ran in a circle around him. A gust sent Grandma's pile of leaves dancing high into the air. A damp leaf slapped Emily in the face, clinging to her skin. She peeled it off and tossed it into the wind.

"Emily, stop!" Christopher yelled again. She didn't look back.

Chapter Forty

Charlotte started walking to the staircase, but the phone rang and she headed back to the kitchen. "Mrs. Stevenson." It was Rayann. "May I please speak to Emily?"

Charlotte climbed the stairs, surprised Emily hadn't answered the phone. She knocked on Emily's door, but there was no answer. She opened the door, but Emily wasn't there. Charlotte was sure she had heard her come in from doing her chores. She knocked on Sam's door, but the only response was his blaring music. She turned the knob. He was on his bed, and there was no sign of the envelope she had seen.

"Emily went outside. She said you were taking her to Ashley's." Sam sat up straight. Charlotte stepped back into the hall. "Rayann, Emily's outside. I'll tell her to call you back.

"Okay." Rayann sounded hesitant, not her usual confident self. "But tell her, first, that I'll call her Sunday evening, okay, to say good-bye after *I* get back from the cabin."

"All right," Charlotte said. What was Rayann up to? Charlotte stopped at the landing window. A whirlwind of leaves flew by. Were those her leaves? She raced downstairs to the backdoor. The wind nearly howled, and the clouds had grown thick and full in just the last half hour. She could hear the chickens in the coop squawking and the rooster crowing. She hoped the thunderstorm would start soon and be done by the time Ashley's party began this evening.

A horn honked. What in the world? Pete drove up the driveway, bouncing old Lazarus up and down. His head hung out the window, but she couldn't hear what he was yelling. Charlotte started to run. Had something happened to Bob?

Pete yelled again. She caught the word "tornado" and kept running toward him.

"There's a tornado warning on the radio. Get the kids to the cellar."

"Where's Dad?" Charlotte shouted as hail began to pound down, drilling her arms and head, bouncing off the ground.

"Probably catching a nap down by the old place. I'm going there now! We'll hunker down there or try to make it back to the house." Pete spun the pickup around and accelerated toward the road.

Had Emily and Christopher come back? She yelled for them. Then she yelled for Toby. Where were they? Maybe the kids had slipped in through the front door. Toby was probably hiding.

She yelled Sam's name as she flung open the front door. He didn't answer. She ran up the stairs, still yelling.

"Grandma!" He stood in his doorway. "What's wrong?"

She was out of breath. "There's a tornado warning. Get to the cellar." She flung open Emily's door. *Please God, please.* No Emily. Charlotte scanned the room. Her overnight bag was *gone*. On the bed was a wadded-up piece of paper. Rayann's words played in Charlotte's head. Something was going on. Charlotte picked up the note. *Cabin. Call Mrs. Matthews. We should be there sometime after 7:30. Love, Emily.*

Sam stood in the doorway to his sister's room.

"When was the last time you saw Emily?"

"I don't know. Ten minutes ago?"

"And Christopher was with her?"

"Well, he was following her down the driveway. I could see them out my window."

Charlotte started for the door. "I'm going after Emily and Christopher. You get to the cellar."

"I'm going too."

"No." Charlotte thundered down the stairs. "Go to the cellar."

Sam followed her out the back door.

"Sam, the cellar!" Charlotte pointed to the house.

"Grandma, I'm going with you." As he spoke, a limb from the maple tree flew across the yard. Charlotte gasped. It bounced against the windshield of her car, shattering the glass, and then landed on the ground. "We'll take Grandpa's pickup!" Sam started running.

"I don't have the key." The clouds in the southwest darkened and churned.

"I'll go get it." Sam raced toward the house.

Charlotte struggled toward the driver's side of the pickup

as the rain pelted down and the wind roared in a frenzy around her. Sam rushed back to the pickup, Bob's key in his hand, and slammed the door after Charlotte climbed in and then ran around to the other side. The windshield wipers couldn't keep up with the fall of water over the glass. If Pete came from the old place and didn't see them, then that meant Emily and Christopher had turned toward town, which made sense. "Dear God," Charlotte prayed, not realizing she'd said it out loud, "Please keep them safe."

"Amen," Sam added.

Pieces of debris—a shingle, a sheet of plastic, the soggy head of a sunflower—hit the windshield one by one, bouncing against the glass and the wipers. She turned onto the highway.

"Why didn't I follow them?" Sam moaned. "I'm supposed to watch out for them."

"They're okay, Sam. We just have to find them."

Charlotte slowed as a piece of siding flew in front of the pickup.

"There it is." Sam pointed out the back window. Charlotte looked in the rearview mirror. The funnel was headed for the road.

Oh, dear God, Charlotte prayed silently, *I can't bear to lose another child. I don't think I could survive losing two.*

Chapter Forty-One

Emily stood in the roadway, soaked through to her skin by the big, fat raindrops that the wind flung against her face along with strands of hair that stung her eyes. She pulled it back with her hand and held on to it tightly. She'd walked at least half a mile, thinking the farther away from the house she met Sean the better. Why hadn't he shown up? Had Sean refused to cooperate? Because he didn't want Emily to go the cabin? The sting of rejection spread into a full-fledged pain in the pit of her stomach. Now she needed to get back because Grandma would be expecting to take her to Ashley's party.

Christopher was yelling something at her, but she couldn't hear him. Maybe Rayann canceled the plan. Emily felt sick. One of them didn't want her along. It hurt. But even though she had decided the plan was a bad idea she still wanted them to come for her.

"Emily!" Christopher's shriek reached her ears. He was by her side, yanking on her arm. Toby shook as she barked and circled around the children. "It's a tornado. I was right."

She wiped her face with her wet hands as the rain stopped and the sky turned an eerie color, almost green.

Emily stopped in her tracks; she had never seen anything like it. "I think we're okay," she said, trying to be brave for Christopher but not believing her own words. Her voice shook. She turned toward Christopher and said, with false hope, "The storm is stopping."

"No! There it is!" Christopher yelled. He pointed back toward the farm, to the right, just a little, down by where Uncle Pete and Grandpa were harvesting. A funnel cloud staggered through the fields like a raging giant. A bank of clouds melded together, forming what looked like a moving, cement wall. Lightning flashed. Emily froze. Toby stopped barking.

The funnel touched down in a plowed field, sucking dust into the twirling wind, turning the cloud a faint brown for a moment, and then as it rose off the ground again, it turned a pinkish shade and lurched forward again. It tilted, like a monstrous mouth, coming after them.

The roaring turned into a high-pitched screech, like a speeding train. Emily clasped her hands over her ears.

The tornado touched down again and toppled a tree. Then the mushrooming top of the cloud spread out, dumping a lawn chair and a piece of metal.

"Jump into the ditch!" Christopher yelled. Toby barked frantically. "Come on, girl." Christopher grabbed Toby by the collar and Emily by her sleeve, yanking on both of them.

What had Emily done? Christopher wouldn't be out here with her if she hadn't been scheming with Rayann in the first place. She knew it was wrong, and she'd done it anyway.

She and Christopher slid down into the ditch, into the muddy water.

"Curl up," Christopher yelled. "Make yourself as little as possible."

Emily wrapped her arm around her brother. Toby, wet and shaking, wiggled her body next to theirs. What would Grandma do if she was with them? Emily began to pray. "God, please keep us safe. And Uncle Pete and Grandpa. And Grandma and Sam." *And Sean. And Rayann*, she added silently, even though right now she was miffed at Rayann.

For a moment, things were quiet and Emily thought about crawling out of the ditch, but then the roar began again, a thundering as if the train racing over the ditch was going to derail on top of them.

Christopher pulled away for a second, untucking his head, lifting his face to the wind.

"Christopher." Emily yelled. The wind stole the word, swallowing it whole. She pulled him back, away from the speeding train.

Leaves and sticks and pebbles and stubble and bits of hay pelted against her skin. She and Christopher huddled together on the bottom of the ditch, clinging to each other.

Chapter Forty-Two

Charlotte slammed on the brakes of Bob's pickup truck, causing it to fishtail on the wet pavement until it slid to a stop. The funnel cloud crossed the road just a hundred yards in front of them.

"Grandma!"

She was sure Sam was shouting but the roar of the tornado made it sound like a whisper. Charlotte pulled the truck to the side of the road and jumped to the pavement, scanning the prairie for her grandchildren. She stepped over a sheet of tin. Ahead, a mangled piece of machinery lay in the middle of the road. Charlotte called out Emily's and Christopher's names.

She cupped her hands around her mouth and yelled again. A strike of lightning flashed in the bank of gray clouds lumbering after the funnel.

Where were the children?

Charlotte started yelling again, and Sam joined her. Perhaps Sean had picked them up. Perhaps they were safe in town. She looked to her right, to the jagged path the tornado had cut through the field. An oak tree lay uprooted on its side, the bumper of a car stuck in the trunk. What if the children had run into the field? Where would they be now?

The funnel cloud turned again and dipped into a gully, disappearing except for the very top which was spreading out quickly, growing thin and faint. The howling eased.

"Emily!" Charlotte screamed. "Christopher!" She paused and then yelled, "Toby!" Maybe the dog *was* with them.

"I hear a bark." Sam started to run.

Charlotte didn't hear anything. Where were they? She scanned the fields to her left and right and then turned and looked the opposite way down the road. Then turned again. Sam stopped.

"It is Toby!" Sam shouted.

This time Charlotte heard the muffled bark too. "Toby!" she yelled.

Another bark and the dog flew to the pavement.

"Emily! Christopher!" Charlotte screamed.

Christopher's head popped out of the ditch. Both she and Sam were running now. Where was Emily? Sam shot toward his brother.

Charlotte's knees nearly buckled as Emily struggled up the bank, her jeans covered in mud, her hair plastered to her face. She turned toward her grandmother, sobbing.

THE STORM STOPPED just as quickly as it had started, leaving a sweet freshness to the air and a vibrant blue sky. "Sam, would you drive home?" Charlotte asked, still clinging to Emily and Christopher. She didn't want to let go of them, not yet. She tossed Sam the keys, surprised to find them in her hand. He caught them and held them up, as if saluting.

Sam drove cautiously down the littered road. Toby sat up front, her nose pressed to the window. Emily couldn't stop crying. "What if something had happened to Christopher?" she sobbed.

"I'm fine." Christopher reached across Charlotte and patted Emily's knee. "Would you stop? I want to tell Grandma about the tornado."

Charlotte wanted to laugh or cry. Or both. "Emily," she said, "calm down."

"I was going to meet Rayann; Sean was going to drive here because she lied to him. I was just going to tell them something, then I was going to Ashley's party."

"I saw your note," Charlotte said.

Emily hiccupped. "I wasn't going to go, Grandma. I changed my mind, totally. I just walked down to the road to tell them that. Honest."

"Grandma, did you see the funnel?" Christopher asked, oblivious to Emily's words.

"Just a second, sweetie." Charlotte turned back to Emily. "But you *were* going to go to the cabin, when I said you couldn't? Earlier today, that had been your plan?"

Emily sobbed again and nodded. "But it was a bad plan. It was Rayann's plan." She rubbed her face with her hands, streaking mud and mascara across her cheeks and forehead.

"But what about you, Emily?"

"I was wrong," she wailed.

"It went over the ditch, just past us," Christopher said. "But then Emily pushed my face into Toby, and I couldn't see anything more. But, Grandma, I wasn't afraid. I knew we were going to be all right."

"I'm sorry." Emily's wail grew louder.

Charlotte leaned her head back and closed her eyes. "Thank you, God."

"Amen," Sam and Christopher chimed in.

"I didn't mean to say that out loud." Charlotte almost laughed as Emily buried her face against her grandmother's neck.

Chapter Forty-Three

Charlotte and the kids stumbled from the pickup a few moments before Pete tore into the driveway, nearly tipping Lazarus over as he took the turn. Charlotte shook her head, relieved and irritated all at once. They were safe, as long as Pete didn't add a wreck to the trauma of the day.

Pete slammed on the brakes and jumped from Lazarus without turning off the ignition. "Is everyone okay?"

"Yes," Charlotte answered. "Is Dad okay?"

"I'm fine." Bob stepped down slowly from the old pickup. "Pete took good care of me." He turned toward Charlotte's car.

"Look." He pointed at Charlotte's smashed windshield.

"I know," Charlotte said. "Thank goodness your keys were in the house."

Pete started toward the kids. Sam and Emily looked dazed, but Christopher ran toward his uncle. "Uncle Pete! I saw the tornado! It passed right in front of us, in front of me and Emily."

"It did?" Pete looked like he was going to cry. "Why weren't you in the cellar?"

Christopher told the story in bits and pieces. Emily's shoulders shook a few times. Pete wrapped his arm around her, and Toby retreated to her doghouse. When Christopher finished the story, Pete wiped the sleeve of his jacket across his face.

"We lost some corn," Bob said matter-of-factly. "Down in the old place quarter. It just missed the combine."

Pete put his head next to Emily's and began to sing, "The house began to pitch, the kitchen took a slitch—"

She hit his arm. "No fair singing movie lines now. I'm too upset."

"How about, 'There's no place like home,'" he whispered, hugging her.

She hit him again but finally started to relax just a little.

Charlotte stood back. Pete had always had a good heart, but having the children around, having someone who needed him, had made it grow. Charlotte patted his back, fighting back her tears.

"It will take less time to finish harvest now, since the tornado had a turn," Pete said and then laughed.

Bob nodded.

"Grandpa, can I drive the truck in the morning?" Sam asked.

Bob chuckled. "That's a fine idea."

"Uh-oh. Look." Christopher pointed toward the cows. "The gate's open."

"Not again." Pete let go of the kids.

The herd was huddled along the far fence.

"Who's missing?" Bob asked. "That little white-faced Houdini?"

Sam ran toward the gate and pulled it shut. "No, he's there by the willow."

Bob began to count. Christopher counted along, softly. "Forty-nine," Christopher proclaimed.

"That's what I got too." Bob counted again. "Yep. They're all there."

"Guess they must have felt safer inside the fence, huh?" Emily said.

The phone rang as Charlotte entered the house. "Mrs. Stevenson, is Emily all right?" Rayann's voice was scratchy.

"Yes, she's fine, but I found her and Christopher down on the road during the worst of the storm."

"I'm sorry." Rayann's voice was a near whisper. "It was my fault, all my idea, but then I changed my mind, because I didn't want Emily to get into trouble. That's when I called before." Rayann paused. "I'm sorry, Mrs. Stevenson."

"Rayann, I forgive you. And Emily too."

"Thank you," Rayann whispered.

"Would you like to talk to her? She's right here."

Emily took the phone. She sounded annoyed as she told Rayann what happened, her change of mind, Christopher following her, and waiting for the Mustang to round the corner.

"Grandma." Emily handed the phone to Charlotte. "Mrs. Matthews wants to talk to you."

After more apologies, Charlotte said good-bye and gave Emily the phone to apologize to Mrs. Matthews.

"Grandma." Emily still held the phone. "I'm going to call Ashley and tell her what happened and that I can't make it to her party. And I'm going to apologize. I know I haven't been a good friend to her."

Charlotte nodded. She didn't need to say a thing. She collapsed into her chair. What she needed was to sit for just a minute. In the end, Emily had done the right thing; so had Rayann, and everyone was safe and mostly sound. Charlotte closed her eyes.

"Grandma." It was Sam.

Charlotte opened her eyes one at a time. He held the envelope in his hand.

"This... it's from where Dad used to, maybe, like, a few years ago." Sam swallowed, his Adam's apple bobbing up and then down. "I was trying to find him."

Charlotte nodded. "I wondered. But you didn't find him?"

Sam shook his head.

"I'm sorry, Sam." She was sorry but also relieved, to be honest. She wasn't against Sam looking, but she wasn't in any hurry for Kevin to be found.

Sam nodded. "It doesn't matter, not now. I just didn't want Uncle Bill to end up being our guardian if something happened to you and Grandpa." He folded the envelope in two and shoved it in his back pocket. "I'm going to go help Pete clean up."

Charlotte gently rocked her chair as Sam left the room. He might not think that it mattered, not after what just happened, but it would matter to him again. There was no stopping it, she knew. She took a deep breath. *Oh, bother.* What *did* she know?

She had been so sure it had been Emily trying to find

their dad. She shouldn't have assumed; she should have asked the children. Hannah had asked if Charlotte prayed for Kevin. She exhaled again. *Okay, Lord*, she said silently, and then she prayed for Kevin.

"COME ON, EMILY. Let's go check on the horses." Charlotte pulled the back door closed.

"We're going to the barn," Emily called out to Christopher as they walked across the lawn. "Want to come with us?"

"Sure."

"If Uncle Bill was our guardian, does that mean that we would leave Heather Creek Farm?" Christopher asked.

"Who told you that?" Charlotte asked.

Christopher shrugged. "I overheard Uncle Bill."

Emily stopped walking. "I don't want to leave here, Grandma."

Charlotte put one hand on Christopher's shoulder and the other on Emily's. Sam and Emily had heard Bill talk about the guardian issue, but she hadn't realized that Christopher had too. "Come here a minute."

Sam jogged toward them, drawing close.

"Listen," Charlotte said, "all three of you. I don't want any of you to give this guardian issue another thought. Grandpa and I will figure this out, and we will keep your best interest in mind. But in the meantime, this is your home."

Pete came out of the doorway that led to his apartment. "Where are you going?" He pulled off his leather work glove and scratched his chin.

"The barn." Emily looped her hair into a bun, securing it with a hair band from her wrist.

"I'll come along." Pete slipped his glove back on his hand. Maybe Pete wouldn't be such a bad influence on these kids after all.

"Hey," Christopher said, "wait for Grandpa."

They turned to see Bob following behind them, and they all slowed until he caught up. Charlotte squeezed his hand.

"Let's stop and pray a minute," Charlotte said. "As a family."

"All right. I'll pray," Bob said. "Dear Lord, we thank thee . . ." They held hands in a circle. Charlotte tried to focus, but her mind kept drifting off. What if Emily and Rayann hadn't changed their minds? Could she have dealt with Emily with grace? Yes. She would have driven to the cabin and brought her home.

Would she have loved her and disciplined her and not been embarrassed when the story leaked out around town? Tears welled in her eyes. She might have remembered, over the years, what Emily had done, but she wouldn't have held it against her.

She wouldn't hold onto hurt from her grandchildren the way she had with her own children. And she would let go of the little hurts, of Bill meddling, of the things that Pete did that disappointed her too. None of that was worth holding on to.

"Amen," Bob said.

"Amen," Charlotte, Pete, and the children echoed.

Christopher wrapped his arms around Charlotte's waist

for just a minute and then took off toward the barn. Toby raced behind, nipping at Christopher's heels. Sam and Pete took off jogging. Bob picked up his pace, as if he thought he could catch the boys and Pete.

But Emily reached for her grandmother's hand, and together they walked side by side toward the barn.

About the Author

Leslie Gould is the author of *Garden of Dreams*, *Beyond the Blue*, and *Scrap Everything*. *Beyond the Blue*, which is about international adoption, was awarded Best Inspirational Novel of the Year by Romantic Times BOOKclub in 2006. Leslie and her husband, Peter, are the parents of four children, ages ten to twenty-one. Leslie is sure that writing and parenting have to be two of the most humbling endeavors in existence, and she hopes that parents of all ages will be encouraged by her novels about family and faith.

A Note from the Editors

This original book was created by the Books and Inspirational Media Division of Guideposts, the world's leading inspirational publisher. Founded in 1945 by Dr. Norman Vincent Peale and Ruth Stafford Peale, Guideposts helps people from all walks of life achieve their maximum personal and spiritual potential. Guideposts is committed to communicating positive, faith-filled principles for people everywhere to use in successful daily living.

Our publications include award-winning magazines such as *Guideposts* and *Angels on Earth*, best-selling books, and outreach services that demonstrate what can happen when faith and positive thinking are applied in day-to-day life.

For more information, visit us at www.guideposts.com, call (800) 431-2344 or write Guideposts, PO Box 5815, Harlan, Iowa 51593.